missing BONES

For further information, contact:
Tumblehome Learning, Inc.
201 Newbury St, Suite 201
Boston, MA 02116
http://www.tumblehomelearning.com
Library of Congress Control Number 2018930838
ISBN 978-1-943431-34-2

Perry, Phyllis J.
Missing Bones / Phyllis J. Perry - 1st ed

Cover Design: Barnas Monteith

Printed in Taiwan
10 9 8 7 6 5 4 3 2 1

missing BONES

Phyllis J. Perry

TUMBLEHOME learning, INC.

CHAPTER 1

"**H**ey! What's wrong, Bones? Are you stuck again?"

Ricky jumped up, bumping the edge of the breakfast table as he hurried across the room. His dog, Bones, was trying hard to squeeze through the tiny cat door leading into the kitchen from the back patio of their new house. Poor Bones. He'd get his head through the little hole, but the rest of his chunky beagle body simply couldn't follow.

"Oh, what's wrong with your dog now?" Annabelle asked, giving an exaggerated sigh, as she came walking into the room. Right behind her, like a black shadow, trailed her cat, Darwin.

Ricky glanced over his shoulder. Why did she have to come waltzing in now? His stepsister was such a pain. Without raising his voice, Ricky managed to say, "Nothing's wrong with *him*. It's that ridiculously small cat door." He bent to help Bones but was too late. Bones had finally figured out there was no way he could squeeze in. So he struggled to back out. He grunted and whined. In the battle to free himself, he pulled off his collar, which fell inside on the floor.

Annabelle laughed. "Dumb dog," she said.

Ricky glared at his stepsister as he opened the patio door.

"Come on in, boy." With tail wagging, Bones followed him into the kitchen. Ricky knelt and put his dog's collar back on. As he patted Bones, Ricky thought, *I know how you feel. You and I don't fit in here, do we? I'm missing our old house in Broomfield, and you are, too, aren't you, old boy?* Bones looked adoringly up at Ricky as if he understood even the unspoken words.

With Bones now out of his way, Darwin paused for a minute in front of his cat door. He lazily stretched and yawned. Then, with a flick of his sleek, black tail, Darwin managed to slap Bones in the nose before disappearing through the door and out into the backyard. Ricky thought how perfectly this evil cat matched its owner.

Annabelle hurried about, pouring herself a bowl of cereal, getting some milk, and then plopping down at the kitchen table. She was dressed for this hot August day wearing pink shorts, a matching tank top, and pink Crocs. Her blonde hair was pulled back in a ponytail and held in place with some sort of hair thingy. Pink, of course.

Without bothering to say anything more, Annabelle began eating, gazing out the window as if she were alone in the room. Ricky walked back to his seat at the table. He started munching again on his piece of toast slathered in peach jam. He didn't bother to say good morning, either. It would be wasted on Annabelle. In the short time they'd been forced to live together in the same house, they had come to an unspoken agreement. When they were alone, arguments and sarcasm were expected. Silence was fine. And there was no reason to waste words being pleasant.

After a few bites of toast, Ricky finally broke the silence. "I thought your dad said he was going to put a new pet door in here so that Bones could go in and out, too."

"He will," Annabelle said. "When he has time. You know he has things to think about other than your old mutt."

"Bones isn't old, and he's not a mutt," Ricky said. "He's a six-year-old thoroughbred beagle, with a great pedigree. This dog has champions behind him."

Annabelle craned her neck, making an exaggerated attempt of trying to look behind Bones for the long line of champions standing behind him. "Right. That's why he has such a distinguished name—Bones." She snorted.

"Well, what sort of name for a cat is 'Darwin'?" Ricky asked.

"A perfectly good name. He's named after Charles Darwin, a great scientist. You've probably never even heard of him. He wrote *The Origin of Species*, all about how animals evolve. In case you haven't noticed, my cat has six toes on each of his front feet. Darwin's a most unusual cat, not a flea-bitten hound."

"My dog's distinguished too," Ricky said, "from a great kennel. I call him Bones, but of course that's not his real name. His registered name is Bayard's Napoleon Bonaparte. He's named after a famous French army commander who you've probably never even heard of."

"Oh, I've heard of him all right. He's the short guy in the funny three-cornered hat who lost the battle at Waterloo." Annabelle grinned in triumph.

Ricky decided to ignore that remark. Score one for Annabelle. Instead, he opened a counter-attack. "What kind of cat is Darwin, anyway?" Ricky stared out the sliding glass door at Darwin, a slender, mostly black cat, with white front paws. "Doesn't look like any special breed to me."

"He's half Siamese," Annabelle remarked hotly.

"And half alley-cat," Ricky added. "Very evolved, if you ask me."

"Well…" sputtered Annabelle, but she was interrupted.

"Good morning, you two," Ricky's mom said, as she entered the room.

Ricky hadn't heard her coming. She wore slippers and a robe. If she'd heard Ricky and Annabelle bickering, she didn't show it.

"Hi, Mom," Ricky said.

"What are you two doing up and dressed so early? I thought you'd be sleeping in, making the most of the last few days of summer. Thursday, it's back to school for all of us."

"I know, Maria," Annabelle said. "But at eight o'clock, they'll post the fifth-grade class lists in front of Mesa School. As soon as I've had breakfast, I'm walking up to find out which teacher I got."

Ricky still couldn't get used to his stepsister calling his mother "Maria." It didn't sound right. Of course, he called his new step-dad "Mike," but that was different. "Maria" sounded weird. Annabelle's mother and father had divorced three years ago, and her mother and her new husband lived in a different state now. Although Annabelle only saw her sometimes during vacations, she still insisted that she could only call her real mother "Mom."

Ricky's dad had died six years ago in a car accident. Ricky had been so little then that although he tried, he could barely picture his dad. For as long as Ricky could remember, it was just Mom, Bones, and him in their comfortable little house in Broomfield.

Then mom met Mike Manders on some school committee last year. They were both teachers in the Boulder Valley schools. They'd dated, and that was okay with Ricky. Mike was a nice guy, and Ricky didn't even mind seeing Annabelle once in a while. Then, this summer, his mom married Mike. Over the weekend, Mom, Ricky, and Bones moved into Mike's house in Boulder. Ricky's old Broomfield house had just been sold. A family called Andrews was moving in this week. That didn't feel right, either.

Ricky hated all the changes—Mike's house, the new neighbors, his stepsister, and that darn step-cat, Darwin. Ricky clung to Bones, his only buddy.

"Oh, right," Mom said. She was busy making a pot of coffee. "Mike told me about the class lists. If you want to wait a few minutes, while I have a cup of coffee and get dressed, I'll drive us up to school to take a look."

"No, thanks," Annabelle said. "It's only a couple of blocks. I'll walk. In fact," she said, glancing at the kitchen clock, "I think I'll leave right now." She slid off her chair.

Ricky's mom said, "Why don't you walk up with her, Ricky? You'll want to know what class you're in, too."

Annabelle looked at Ricky. He could read the dismay written all over her face, and he actually felt sorry for her. She was a pain, but probably the only one who halfway understood how he felt. He was sure she hadn't wanted a stepbrother any more than he'd wanted a stepsister. Hadn't his mother and Mike seen that yet? Love really must be blind.

Ricky quickly said, "Thanks, but I'm going to have another piece of toast. I may walk up later, or not. I'm in no big rush."

Annabelle looked relieved. "See you later," she called as she rushed through the front door, obviously glad to escape.

Ricky's mother looked as if she were about to say something, but before she did, Mike came walking in, freshly shaved, showered, and dressed. "Good morning," he said. He stepped up behind Ricky's mother and gave her a kiss on the back of her neck. Then he asked, "Where's Belle? I thought I heard her talking."

"You just missed her," Ricky's mother said. "Annabelle went hurrying off to school to find out which teacher she got and which friends are going to be in her class."

Mike glanced at the clock. "It's only a quarter to eight. I was going to take her up. She'll be there before the lists are even out."

"I already offered to drive her," Ricky's mom said, "but she was anxious to go on her own. She's probably expecting to meet some of her friends up there."

"How about you, Ricky?" Mike asked. "Don't you want to find out which teacher you have?"

"No big deal," Ricky said. "I don't know any of the teachers, and other than George up the street, I don't know any of the kids, either."

Mike said, "This is tough on you, Ricky. After being in the same school in Broomfield since kindergarten, you have to switch schools. But you'll like fifth grade at Mesa. You'll make new friends in no time."

"Yeah," Ricky said as convincingly as he could. To avoid further conversation, he got up and made himself another piece of toast.

Darwin came back through the cat door and gave a little meow.

"Did Belle go off and forget to give you breakfast?" Mike asked. He poured some milk into Darwin's cat bowl.

Ricky felt like asking, "Instead of wasting time on that silly cat, why don't you put in a new pet door?" But he swallowed the words along with his second piece of toast. Then he opened the door and walked out into the backyard. Bones trailed after him.

Ricky picked up the old ball that was sitting on the ground where he'd left it yesterday and gave it a short toss. Immediately, Bones sprang into the air and caught it. He brought it back to Ricky, dropped it, and then danced off a few feet, keeping his eye on Ricky. This time Ricky gave it a long toss, and Bones raced off and caught it neatly. For the next half-hour, Ricky played with his dog.

Then the two of them sat down together on the patio. "Good dog," Ricky said, ruffling his dog's fur. "How'd you like to take a walk? We could take a hike up Mole Hill this morning before it gets really hot." Mole Hill was the name Ricky had given to a small hill on Open Space land located just behind the school, leading up into the mountains. The trailhead was only about ten blocks away.

It was one of the few pluses about living here. Ricky was an outdoors person. He had learned a lot about identifying the prints of wild animals, recognizing birds and their calls, and identifying rocks, trees, and wild flowers. He and Bones had walked along a stream in Broomfield, and he was glad that there was Open Space land near Mike's house in Boulder where they could hike.

Ricky tromped back inside with Bones. He was just telling his mom that he and Bones were going for a short hike when Annabelle banged through the front door. She ran to the kitchen. On her face was a scowl.

"What's wrong, Belle?" Mike asked.

Annabelle seemed to be trying hard to hold back tears. Between sniffs and sighs, and with trembling lip, she pointed a finger straight at Ricky and shouted, "Him. He's what's wrong."

CHAPTER 2

M ike stood up, and Annabelle ran straight into his arms, releasing a flood of tears.

"Honey, what is it? What did Ricky do?" Mike asked. As the sniffling and trembling continued, Mike gently led Annabelle into the living room, sat on the couch, and held her close.

Ricky and his mother stood in the kitchen exchanging awkward glances. Ricky wondered if his mother felt as confused and uncomfortable as he did. He felt more like a stranger looking on than part of the family. Then Mom reached out her hand, took Ricky's, and led him into the living room, too.

By this time Annabelle's sniffs and sighs were lessening a little. Mom sat on the couch on the other side of Annabelle and put one hand gently on her arm. Ricky flopped into one of the chairs. Bones followed Ricky in and lay down at his feet. Somehow, as Ricky looked across the room, he felt that an unseen battle line was drawn—Mom, Mike, and Annabelle on one side, Ricky and Bones on the other.

Annabelle finally managed to choke out a few words. "They posted the class lists, and at first I was really happy. Kelly is in the same room with me, and I got Mr. Bennett." She looked up at her father, and a small smile sneaked across her tear-stained face and then disappeared.

"Hey, that's great," Mike said. "Your best friend in the same class and the teacher you told me you thought you'd like. So what's the problem?"

Annabelle's lip trembled. "They put Ricky in the same class with me. That's the problem." She looked over at where Ricky sat and glared.

Oh, no, Ricky thought. *Not stuck in the same classroom with her. That would definitely be cruel and unusual punishment.* But he said nothing.

Annabelle continued her complaint. "I know we have to live together, but do we have to be in the same classroom together all day long? You know they never put twins in the same room, so why would they put us together?"

"You don't have the same last name," Mike explained. "Ricky's new, and the secretary didn't realize that you two are brother and sister."

"Stepbrother and sister," Ricky corrected him.

Mike gave Ricky a quick look before turning back to Annabelle. Then he shot another glance at Ricky and asked, "What do you think about all this, Ricky?"

Ricky thought this might be one of the few times he'd ever agreed with his stepsister about anything. He spoke right up. "Annabelle's right. We don't want to be in the same classroom together all day."

Mike and Ricky's mother exchanged uneasy glances. Ricky wondered if this was the first moment they realized all was not happiness in this new family.

"Well, that's easy to fix," Mike went on. "I'll phone the office right now. I can probably make the change over the phone, but if we need to, we'll go up and talk with them. I'm sure they'll make a switch."

Annabelle brightened immediately at this good news and began to dry off her face with the back of her hand.

"Who are the other fifth grade teachers?" Ricky asked.

"There are only two fifth grade classes this year," Mike said, looking first at Ricky and then over Annabelle's head at his wife as he spoke. "Mr. Bennett and Mrs. Hannigan. Mr. Bennett was new to the school last year, and he fit in right away. He's young and eager, works hard, and everyone seems to like him. Annabelle was really hoping to get him."

He looked back down at Annabelle, brushing her hair back from her face and went on. "And there's Mrs. Hannigan." Mike looked back up at Ricky. "She's been at the school for a long time, and she's really good."

Ricky looked over at Annabelle, who squirmed a little in her seat and suddenly dropped her gaze. A dead give-away. Clearly Annabelle did not think Mrs. Hannigan was a prize. More likely she was an old battle-axe. Annabelle, the drama queen, knew that by turning on a few tears, she'd be rid of Ricky, be with her best friend, and get the prize teacher, too. Well, maybe not.

Ricky spoke up. "I'd like to stay in Mr. Bennett's class. It sounds as if he'd be a lot more fun. You can move, Annabelle."

Ricky enjoyed watching Annabelle suddenly jerk up her head. Score one for Ricky. Annabelle hadn't been expecting that.

"But Kelly's in Mr. Bennett's class. I'd be missing my best

friend and not get the teacher I wanted." She stared pleadingly at Ricky. This time, it was Ricky who dropped his gaze.

He was being mean and he knew it, but he didn't care. Looking down at the floor, Ricky muttered, "Well, I'm missing my town, my house, my school and all my friends." Then Ricky glared at his stepsister and set his jaw.

No one said anything for a moment, but Ricky watched his mother and Mike exchange glances. Then his mother looked at Ricky.

She didn't seem mad, just sad. And she didn't say anything or accuse him of anything. As a matter of fact, Ricky wished she would, but his mom wasn't like that.

It was very quiet in the room.

Gradually Ricky's jaw unclenched. He finally spoke. "I guess Annabelle should get to stay with her friend in Mr. Bennett's class. Go ahead and move me. I don't know the teachers or anybody up at Mesa anyway. No point in both of us being miserable."

Ricky saw the look of relief exchanged between Mike and his mother, and the smile that suddenly blossomed on Annabelle's face. He wished he could take some joy from it, but he couldn't. Ricky knew that offering to switch should make him feel good, like a hero, but it didn't. In fact, he felt like crying too. Suddenly he felt he had to get out of here.

Ricky stood up quickly, and Bones immediately scrambled to his feet too. "Bones and I are going for a walk, Mom. We'll be back by lunch." Ricky headed for the front door.

"Hey, hang on a minute," Mike said. He looked uncomfortable. "Are you sure about this? You'd be okay changing to Mrs. Hannigan's class?"

"Yeah," Ricky said. "Whatever." After all, he thought to himself, what choice did he really have? His mother had had a long talk with him before she agreed to marry Mike and make the move to Boulder. Ricky wanted her to be happy, and he'd said he'd do his best to make things work. He hadn't realized then how hard this would be.

Ricky stopped short when his mother called, "Ricky, don't forget the leash."

He turned and this time went out of the house through the garage door. Just outside that door, Ricky stopped to pick up the leash that hung on a nail there. That was another thing about this new town that he didn't like. In Broomfield, you and your dog could go for a walk anywhere you wanted without a leash. Dogs only had to be under voice control. Here in Boulder, all dogs had to be on leash in the city. You had to take a course and get a special tag for your dog to be unleashed on Open Space land. It was the law. Ricky hadn't had a chance to take the course yet.

Angrily, Ricky fastened the leash onto Bones' collar. He took a minute to clip onto his belt the water bottle that also hung there. It had an extra plastic cup attached with a short length of chain. He knew he should go inside and fill the bottle with fresh water, but he wanted to get away. He couldn't stand to face everyone again. Ricky grabbed his baseball cap that hung on another nail and tugged it onto his head. Then he set off at a good clip.

In a couple of blocks when Ricky neared Mesa School, he noticed the knot of kids crowded around a tack board that had been rolled outside onto the sidewalk. Papers were pinned to it. No doubt these were the class lists. Instead of going up the sidewalk to the school, Ricky turned to the right and then took a cross street that led to the trailhead.

Once on the piece of Open Space called Bear Canyon, they walked a short distance on a path through some shrubs to the little wooden bridge that crossed Bear Creek. On this hot August morning, there wasn't more than a trickle of water in the creek. At the edge of the creek, Ricky saw animal tracks. He bent down for a closer look. Deer tracks. No doubt about it. Pulling out his smart phone, Ricky snapped a picture for his collection. Crossing the bridge, Ricky turned to the left and started up a narrow winding trail that led to the top of Mole Hill.

Suddenly, he saw a movement in one of the bushes. Bones saw it, too, and pulled in that direction. Ricky held the leash firmly while staring in the bush. He heard the familiar call, "Chewink!" Then he spied it. A rufous-sided towhee. The bird fluttered, and went deeper into the bush. But not before Ricky had caught a glimpse of its red eye.

As they continued walking, shrubs were left behind. This area was wide open. Tall brown grass, dried from months of summer sun, created a broad golden mound. If you squinted just right, you might think you were looking at a sand dune.

Ricky kept thinking about the scene he had just left. Annabelle and her tears, Mike looking worried, his mother looking sad. Hey! News flash. Were the lovebirds finally realizing that their little nest wasn't filled with pure joy? Ricky gritted his teeth. He knew he had to make the best of it for his mom's sake. He was willing to take Mike, the new house, new school, and new friends. But drama queen Annabelle? And that dumb cat, Darwin? That was too much.

Ricky and Bones climbed to the very top of Mole Hill without pausing along the way, and then both sat down. Ricky unclipped his water bottle. It was only half full. He took a long gulp. The water was warm and stale tasting. Even so, Ricky was glad for the drink. He poured some water into the extra cup, and Bones drank, too.

Ricky tried to push all thoughts of his new stepfamily from his mind. He scratched the special spot behind Bones' ear as he stared from his high perch down at the town below. For a moment, they both sat there, contented. The hot sun baked down on them. Ricky felt some of the tightness ooze out of his body. He took another drink and poured out what was left of the water for Bones, who eagerly lapped it up.

"Okay, boy, time to head back. It's too hot to sit up here without any shade." They set off down the trail. It was a lot faster and easier going down, and they made good time. When they drew close to Mesa School, Ricky noticed that there was no longer a crowd. Everyone must have already come and gone. Ricky walked up the sidewalk leading to the school and looked at the lists.

By this time, the printed sheets showed a few changes that had been neatly lettered in ink. Ricky looked at the fifth grade list for Mrs. Hannigan. A name had been added, squeezed right in between the names of Lombard and Nelson. Neatly printed there was Martinez, Ricardo. He didn't notice any other Hispanic names. There was no Barilla, Garcia, or Fernandez.

Next, Ricky checked out Mr. Bennett's fifth grade class list. A neat line had been drawn through, Martinez, Ricardo. It gave him a funny feeling seeing his name crossed out like that. Sort of like he wasn't here any more.

He idly glanced at the Hannigan list again and noted that Schumacher, George, was in the same class with him. *One familiar face,* Ricky thought. George lived across the street and three houses up. Ricky had only seen him one time, riding his bike down the street. George had come by just as Ricky and Mike were getting into the car. Mike had waved and called out, "Hi, George."

George had stopped, and Mike had introduced the two boys. George was a tall, skinny kid much like Ricky. But while Ricky's hair was dark brown like his mother's, George's hair was light blond. George soon sped on his way. Mike told Ricky that George had an older brother, named Jeff, who was a freshman in high school.

A couple of times after that when Ricky had been walking by, he'd heard saxophone sounds coming from George's house. Ricky paid attention because he had taken trumpet lessons for a while in Broomfield. Once the saxophone player in George's house sounded really good and Ricky was impressed. Another time, he sounded awful.

Ricky looked again at the list. All those names in his class, and he knew only one person. He gave a little tug on the leash and Bones, who'd been checking out something in the shrubs near by the front of the school, looked up, ready to go. The two of them left the school and walked the few blocks toward home.

As they walked past George's house, Ricky was careful to keep his eyes pointed straight ahead. If George was at home and saw him pass by, Ricky didn't want George to think he was checking him out. Ricky didn't want to look desperate for a friend. Even if he was.

CHAPTER 3

The first day of the new school year started on Thursday. Ricky thought this was another dumb idea, typical of this dumb town, and he said so at breakfast that morning.

"Why don't they just start on Monday?" he grumbled. At least, that would put off this misery of being the new kid in the new school for four more days.

Of course, Annabelle saw things differently. "I'm just glad they waited until Thursday. That gave us three more days of vacation this week."

Ricky didn't bother to explain he meant next Monday, not last Monday. He didn't know if his new stepsister thought starting on a Thursday really was a good idea, or whether she was taking the opposite opinion simply to get to him.

"Hey, remember that the teachers already started back on Tuesday," Ricky's mother chimed in. "So no complaints from you." She smiled at Ricky as she spoke. "Actually, I've needed every minute to get ready to meet my students today. You kids think it's hard to go back, but let me tell you, it's not a picnic for teachers, either."

"You're right about that," Mike added.

While she spoke, Ricky's mom poked a hollow in the salsa and beans simmering in the skillet, added four eggs, and covered the skillet. A few minutes later she announced, "The *huevos rancheros* are ready."

"Thanks, but no thanks," Annabelle said. She coolly went and poured some cereal into a bowl, adding milk. On several earlier occasions, Annabelle had already made her eating choices clear. "That's way too spicy to start out the day," Annabelle commented and she sat and began eating her cereal.

Ricky's mother said nothing as she dished up the *huevos rancheros* for the rest of them.

"It's special," Ricky said. "I always have it on the first day of school. You don't know what you're missing."

Annabelle just sniffed her disapproval.

Conscious of the time, everyone ate quickly this morning with little conversation.

Mike glanced at the kitchen clock. "I've got to get going. I've got farther to go than the rest of you." He pushed back from the table and carried his dishes over to the sink.

He turned back toward the kids. "Remember, since you've got a ton of school supplies to lug up there today, Mrs. Schumacher said she'd give you a ride. After today, you can walk on your own. Be sure you're out on the porch to meet her at seven-thirty. Don't make her wait."

Ricky's mother stood, too. "You've got your supplies and lunch money, so I think you're both set. Let's all have a great day!"

Within a few minutes, both parents had driven off. Annabelle and Ricky quickly and silently cleaned up their breakfast things, and then went about getting themselves ready for school. Of course Annabelle galloped up the stairs first and monopolized the bathroom—another thing that irked Ricky. She practically lived in there. He got exactly two minutes in the bathroom before he had to run downstairs to meet Mrs. Schumacher.

They waited only briefly on the porch before Mrs. Schumacher appeared with George sitting beside her on the front seat. George turned his head and said, "Hi." No welcoming smile, Ricky noticed, but at least he spoke. That put him way ahead of Annabelle.

Annabelle said hi back, but Ricky noticed she didn't smile, either. Clearly these two weren't great friends, which immediately raised George in Ricky's estimation.

"It's a bummer that vacation's over, isn't it?" Ricky said.

George turned around and smiled in full agreement. "Yeah. And it's still so hot. Boy, I wish I could go swimming at the pool this afternoon instead of doing math problems. Do you swim?"

"At the Rec Center in Broomfield," Ricky said. "They've got a great twisty slide."

"We've got one of those at the Boulder Rec Center too," George said. "It's like a corkscrew. You'll have to try it out sometime."

Annabelle remained silent during this exchange with a bored look pasted on her face. Ricky wondered if she really was bored or just irritated at being left out of the conversation. Mrs. Schumacher made a few friendly comments as they drove the few blocks.

When they reached the school parking lot, the kids gathered up their bags and backpacks and climbed out. Annabelle didn't hang around. With a hurried "thanks" to Mrs. Schumacher, she totally ignored Ricky and George as she ran toward the playground, meeting and greeting friends as she went.

George waved goodbye to his mother and took his time ambling off toward a clump of boys standing near the back door to the school. Ricky mumbled, "Thanks," and stood uncertainly outside the car door. Then George turned his head and looked back and to

Ricky's relief made a signal with his hand to follow.

George and a big red-headed boy leaned against the back corner of the building. Neither one looked any happier than Ricky felt. Then a short, chubby, sandy-haired kid came puffing up.

"Hey, Wally," George said. "Meet Ricky, my new neighbor."

Wally smiled at Ricky and said, "Hi," with genuine enthusiasm. Then he looked back at George and said, "Hey! I think you grew another six inches this summer. What's the weather like up there?"

He crouched down as if looking up at a skyscraper and laughed loudly at his own joke.

When the bell rang, Wally jerked his head toward the building and said to Ricky, "This way. Let us lead you to your doom." He grinned as he said this.

Ricky tagged along behind George and Wally into the building. The red-head walked off in a different direction. It felt strange not to know where he was going. With a pang, Ricky thought of Heritage School in Broomfield where he knew every nook and cranny.

The boys walked down a long hall to room fifteen. Ricky, George, and Wally each claimed a seat in the back, as far from the teacher as possible. It was probably too much to hope that they'd get to keep these choice seats, but Ricky thought it was a great place to start.

Ricky stared in some surprise at the teacher. While she wasn't young, Mrs. Hannigan wasn't as old as Ricky thought she might be. He had imagined a pale, white-haired hunchback with very thick glasses and a cane. Actually, Mrs. Hannigan was tall and thin, with short, dark hair, streaked with a little gray, and she had a dark tan as if she'd spent a lot of the summer out in the sun.

Mrs. Hannigan started out the morning with a cheerful greeting and soon started giving lots of short assignments, mostly review. The morning passed quickly. Work wasn't too hard or too easy. Ricky caught a glimpse of Annabelle in the cafeteria at noon, but they didn't speak or acknowledge each other.

That afternoon, Ricky met the P.E. teacher, Mr. Cendalli, whom everyone called 'Mr. C.' The class went to the far end of the field for a short baseball game. A girl and a boy were made captains and chose teams. Ricky wasn't too surprised to be the last boy picked. And even then he wasn't called by name but as "you, the new kid." Ricky felt his face grow hot. He hated this place where he was nameless. Still, he tried to play his best. He hit a long ball when he was up at bat, and he caught a fly out in center field. *Maybe next time*, Ricky thought, *I'll only be the next to last pick.*

After they finished playing, Mr. C made a point of calling out loudly, "Hey, Ricky. Give me a hand with these, will you?"

Ricky trotted over and helped carry a sack of bats and balls back to the gym.

"You a baseball fan?" Mr. C asked as they walked along.

"Yeah," Ricky said, and added, "the Yankees are my team." He waited for a groan.

"Hey! Mine, too."

Ricky took an immediate liking to Mr. C. First, Mr. C knew his name. And Yankee fans were few and far between in Colorado where everyone was mad for the Rockies.

All in all, the first day wasn't bad. Friday was much the same. Mrs. Hannigan said that they would be investigating and writing a report about some career in which they were interested. They were to write a five-hundred-word report which should include information they got from talking to someone who worked in that field. Ricky thought he could ask his mom about teaching, but he'd have to admit he really didn't want to be cooped up in a classroom. Still, that report was a long way off. He'd think about it some other time.

They went to their general music class. Near the end of the period, Ricky was handed a sign-up form for instrumental music. Two teachers from the nearest middle school would be coming to Mesa on Tuesday and Thursday afternoons to teach instrumental music to the Mesa fourth and fifth graders, strings in one section and all the other instruments in the second section.

"Are you going to play saxophone the in the band?" Ricky asked George as they walked down the hall back to class.

"Yeah. How did you guess that?"

"A couple times when I walked by your house, I heard you playing."

"Maybe you heard me, or maybe you heard my brother," George said. "He plays saxophone, too, at the high school." Then he grinned. "If what you heard sounded good, it was me! Do you play an instrument?"

"Trumpet."

"Going to play in the Mesa band?"

"Maybe," Ricky said. Actually, he wasn't even sure where his trumpet was. He kind of liked playing it, and he had taken lessons for a while. But he'd never played in a band, and he hadn't touched his trumpet in months. In fact, Ricky hadn't seen it anywhere since the move. But it had to be around somewhere.

Would he like to be in a band? It sounded kind of fun. But then Ricky frowned. He didn't know if Annabelle played an instrument or not. If she did, no doubt she wouldn't want him to be in the same band. There'd be another night featuring the drama queen. Ricky would check it out tonight, but he already knew that he'd rather not play than go through another big Annabelle scene again.

CHAPTER 4

The last hour of the day on Friday turned out to be the most interesting one of the week. Mrs. Hannigan explained that she reserved this hour for what she called a class meeting.

"It's a time each week we can plan events or problem solve," she said. "Today, we have a trip to plan—our Outdoor Education weekend."

A general murmur raced through the class. Ricky, as a newcomer, had no clue as to what this was all about.

"Each year the fifth graders leave on a Friday and go to Camp Betasso," Mrs. Hannigan said. "It's an Outdoor Education area jointly owned by several school districts. This year Mesa got the early draw. We have the camp for the weekend of August 27th and 28th. A bus will pick us up here at school next Friday morning and bring us back home again on Saturday after lunch."

Hey! An overnight trip! Ricky loved camping and being outdoors, and science was his favorite subject.

"At Betasso, there are small cabins with bunk beds where we'll spend the night. A couple of the cabins sleep six. Most sleep four boys or four girls to a cabin. It's great to be going early this year, but we've got to get organized quickly."

Mrs. Hannigan walked over to her desk and picked up a stack of papers that she handed out. Quickly she led them through the packet. There was a long list of things to bring, like flashlights, hats, and hiking shoes. And there was a short list of what not to pack. A few groans went up from some corners of the room as students learned that iPods, iPhones, and electronic games were to stay at home.

"Mr. Bennett and I will be there, of course," Mrs. Hannigan said.

Oh, no, Ricky thought. Both fifth grade classes were going? Even out camping would he be stuck with Annabelle? What a downer. And she probably hated the out-of-doors. She'd be afraid of spiders, and she certainly wouldn't want to do anything that chipped her precious fingernails.

"Other adults will join us," Mrs. Hannigan continued. "One will lead a nature art class, a botanist will talk about plants and trees. I'm teaching a class using microscopes and pond water. Mr. Bennett is the expert on orienteering. There will be a couple of hikes.What we do on Friday evening is wide open; so I need your best ideas. Then I'll check with Mr. Bennett to see what his kids come up with."

"What do kids usually do up there on Friday nights?" Wally asked.

"One year, we held a talent show. Kids sang, danced, and played instruments. One year we held a sing-along. Another year we invited a storyteller to come and tell ghost stories." She paused for a moment and thought. "Once we made popcorn and watched a movie."

Mrs. Hannigan looked up at the clock. It read 2:15. "Tell you what. There are twenty-eight of you. Why don't you gather in cabin groups, four or six kids in a group? Pick out an animal name for your cabin group. You know, tigers, eagles, and barracudas, whatever. Then try to come up with at least one idea for Friday night."

Ricky felt really nervous. He'd been the last boy picked for a baseball team. What if no one wanted him to be in their cabin? Why should they? He hardly knew anyone. Trying to keep his cool, Ricky looked over at George and then at Wally. He plunged ahead. "Want to be in the same cabin?"

"Sure," George agreed.

"Yeah," Wally said.

Ricky hadn't realized till then that he'd been holding his breath. The boys pulled their chairs closer together forming a cabin group. Should they find a fourth, try to join with three others, or just wait? Since he really didn't know anyone else, Ricky decided the next move was up to George and Wally.

It was George who called, "Hey, Yan. Want to share a cabin with us?"

"Okay." Yan dragged his chair over to join them.

As simple as that, Ricky was in a cabin group of four. As they talked, Ricky found that he liked Yan, who was black-haired and tiny. He wore glasses which gave him a serious look. In a whispered huddle they soon came up with a cabin name—Owls. As Wally explained, "This gives us an excuse to stay up all night."

"Any ideas for Friday night?" George asked.

No one spoke for a bit. Then Ricky said, "What about a Magic Night?"

"Cool," Wally said. "Do you do magic?"

"I know a few tricks," Ricky said. "Probably a lot of other kids do, too. It could sort of be Open Magic Night. People could sign up to do their best trick."

"I know a trick," Yan said. "A pretty good one, too."

"It's a great idea," George said. "Way more fun than a sing-along. But a few magic tricks wouldn't last very long."

"I could ask a professional magician to perform, too," Ricky offered. "Marko the Magnificent lives in Broomfield where I used to live. He comes to birthday parties and things like that. My mom knows him, and I think he'd come if he's not booked up."

"Great," Yan said.

Finally it was time for each cabin group to give its name and offer suggestions to Mrs. Hannigan. The boys' cabins were named Owls, Rattlers and Grizzlies. The girls chose Cougars, Hawks and Chipmunks.

After hearing all the ideas for Friday night, the kids voted. Magic Night was their first choice. Ricky couldn't help but feel kind of proud. It was his job over the weekend to see if Marko would really come. Mrs. Hannigan said she'd check with Mr. Bennett on their favorite idea, and then the two fifth grades would vote between the two choices on Monday.

That started Ricky worrying. If Annabelle found out that Magic Night was his idea, Ricky was sure she'd turn all her friends against it. He'd have to play it cool and not let on that it was his idea. Could he convince Mom to snag the magician and keep Annabelle in the dark?

Ricky wondered what had happened in Annabelle's class. She probably suggested that they hold a fashion show on Friday night. He could picture her at dinner tonight, monopolizing the conversation as usual. She'd tell all about her wonderful cabin group, probably called the Peacocks, and their wonderful idea for Friday night.

In spite of dreading dinner with Annabelle, Ricky felt pretty good as he headed home alone. Mom and Mike never actually said that Annabelle and Ricky should walk together to and from school, so of course they didn't. Annabelle had left first this morning. What chance did Ricky have even if he wanted to leave earlier? He couldn't ever get in the bathroom.

And Annabelle was the last to get home yesterday, and she probably would be every day. She and her friends were forever hanging around and talking, talking, talking. Ricky probably could have waited and walked with George, but he didn't. He thought it was up to George to make the first move. Ricky zipped out the school door right at three o'clock.

Today had been really hot, and this afternoon there were rumbles in the sky. Boulder often had heavy thunder showers late in the day in August. Ricky was less than a block from home when a streak of lightning came zigzagging toward the ground. In a few seconds there was the rumble of thunder. Ricky looked up at the threatening sky and quickened his pace. He didn't want to get caught in a rain storm, and he was worried about Bones.

Bones was a brave dog most of the time, but he was terrified of thunder. He also couldn't stand the fireworks that went off around the Fourth of July. At such times, Bones hid under the bed.

Thinking of his dog, Ricky started jogging down the hill. The moment he got home, Ricky dropped his backpack and ran to the back patio door. Bones was outside, whining, poking his nose into the cat door, and scratching at it. Ricky scowled. Mike still hadn't made the door bigger.

Quickly, Ricky slid open the door and let Bones inside. His dog wiggled all over and licked Ricky's hands.

"Hey! I haven't been gone that long," Ricky said as Bones continued dancing round his feet. "Do you want a treat, boy?"

Ricky got him a hard, bone-shaped biscuit that was a favorite.

"Someday," Ricky said, leaning over to give Bones his treat, "Mike will get around to putting in a door that's big enough for you, I hope."

There was another loud clap of thunder. Bones dropped his biscuit and hightailed it up the stairs heading for Ricky's bedroom. Hearing someone at the front door, and realizing it must be Annabelle, Ricky halfway wished he could join Bones hiding under the bed.

Chapter 5

When his mom got home from teaching, Ricky found a chance to get her alone for a minute in the kitchen to talk to her. He told her about the upcoming overnight camping trip.

"Would you call Marko the Magnificent, Mom, and ask if he'd come perform for us, up at the Outdoor Ed camp? He'd be so great."

"Of course I will. He usually charges for shows, but since this is a special school outing, he might be willing to do it for free. It could be good advertising for him."

"And Mom," Ricky went on. "Could this be our secret for now?"

His mother looked puzzled. "Secret?"

"Yeah. I mean until we know for sure, will you please not share with Annabelle and Mike the possibility of a magic show?"

His mother frowned. "Why do we need to keep it a secret, Ricky?"

"Just till Monday," Ricky said. "I mean nothing's definite. We don't know if the kids will vote to have a magic show. And we don't know if Marko will be able to come, or if he'd do it for free. I'd feel stupid suggesting it and getting everyone all excited if it's not going to happen. Can't we wait until you find out if Marko can come, and see how the kids vote Monday? Once it's for sure, we can tell Annabelle and Mike all about it."

His mother looked puzzled, but she agreed, and she immediately went to her study and phoned her magician friend.

Ricky waited anxiously in the kitchen. When she came back, smiling, his mom reported, "Mark says he'd love to do it and won't charge. He thinks it would be good publicity and might get him some business in the future at Boulder kids' parties."

"You explained that we won't know for sure until Monday?" Ricky asked.

"Yes," Ricky's mom said. "I told him I'd call him Monday night and let him know."

Ricky breathed a sigh of relief. So far, so good. His idea for a Magic Night at the Outdoor Ed weekend stood a really good chance.

At dinner, Ricky's mother and stepdad both shared a few funny stories about their work week. Both of them thought they had good classes and were excited about the start of the new year. Ricky tossed in a word or two about really liking the P.E. teacher, but it was Annabelle who did most of the talking.

She went on and on about the Outdoor Education weekend that was coming up. "I'm going to be in the same cabin with Kelly and Christa and Beth. We're the Butterflies. Isn't that a great name? We've all agreed to wear pink PJs."

Ricky managed not to laugh out loud. He just quietly swallowed a forkful of mashed potatoes without choking and took a big drink of milk.

"Of course I have some pink PJs," Annabelle went on, "But I wondered if maybe I could get a new pair for the trip? Something special? Maybe with butterflies?"

"I think we could go on a short shopping trip," Ricky's mom said. "Maybe late tomorrow morning?"

"It's going to be so much fun!" Annabelle babbled on. "Michelle Jenkins went last year, and I remember her telling me about it. She says there's a little pond and that in the summer it's crowded with these amazing water lilies, white and pink. I can't wait to see them."

During dessert, Annabelle said, "Oh, and we're going to be writing a report about careers. It won't be due for a couple of weeks. I'm not really sure what I'd like to do, something that's not boring."

Ricky managed not to roll his eyes. He hoped Annabelle might mention what her class had discussed for Friday night entertainment, but she didn't say, and he didn't dare ask. He couldn't look overly interested in that topic. He didn't want to make her suspicious. Since she didn't mention it, Ricky thought whatever it was, it probably wasn't her idea, or even one of her friends' ideas, so she wouldn't have any special interest in it.

"What about you, Ricky?" his mom asked. "What are you going to explore for a career?"

"I don't know," Ricky admitted. "Something to do with animals, maybe. I haven't thought about it much yet. But definitely some kind of science work outdoors."

The subject of instrumental music came up, too. "I've got a form for you to sign, Dad," Annabelle said. "It gives me permission to take music this year. Kelly and I are both going to be playing violin in the orchestra. It'll be so much fun."

"How about you, Ricky?" his mother asked. "Are you interested in the Mesa band or orchestra?"

Before he could say a word, Annabelle quickly asked, "You don't play violin, do you?"

"No," Ricky answered. "Trumpet."

Ricky saw Annabelle visibly relax. Apparently she didn't care if he played in the band, just so long as he wasn't in "her" orchestra.

"Is my trumpet around somewhere, Mom?" Ricky asked.

"Of course it is," his mother said. "As a matter of fact, I believe you'll find it on the shelf in your closet."

After the table was cleared, as Ricky walked upstairs to look in his closet, he smiled inwardly. He had avoided the Battle of the Bands, and he had a magic secret that Annabelle knew nothing about.

He picked up his trumpet but didn't play it. Instead, he switched on his small radio to his favorite music station, KBNO, and listened to some great Mexican music. Annabelle always complained when he turned it on, or simply turned up her own favorites louder. But she was still downstairs tonight, yakking it up, so he could lie back and enjoy it.

CHAPTER 6

Saturday morning, Ricky and his mother were up by seven. Even on weekends, they were early risers, and Ricky was glad. It meant there was no one in the kitchen except the two of them. It felt like old times. Mom fixed them both scrambled eggs, and after they'd eaten, Ricky told his mother that he and Bones were going for a long hike.

"I want to leave early before it gets hot," Ricky said. "I'm going to explore the Bear Mountain Trail. I checked it out on the city's Open Space map. Looks like a good hike. I'll be home around two."

"Okay," his mother agreed. "Going alone?"

Ricky shot her a look. Was she really expecting him to ask Annabelle to go with him?

His mother quickly said, "I thought maybe George might like to join you. For company."

"No, just me and Bones," Ricky said. He left unsaid the fact that he wasn't sure George would want to go hiking with him. "That's all the company I need."

"Well, have a good time. Annabelle and I will go shopping about ten o'clock, I think, but we'll be home before you are."

Ricky got out a loaf of bread and started making sandwiches and then got some baggies, filling one with Oreo cookies and the other with dog biscuits. He hurried out into the garage, got the water bottle, and filled it with ice water from the fridge. After adding an apple and a power bar, he put all his supplies in a small day pack.

Bones, who had been resting nearby, head down on his paws, watched Ricky's comings and goings with interest. Something, maybe it was the day pack, or maybe the water bottle, signaled they were about to go for a walk. Bones scrambled to his feet and began following Ricky about, getting underfoot.

By eight o'clock, Mike and Annabelle still hadn't appeared in the kitchen. Ricky grabbed the leash in the garage, and he and Bones headed off. Bones didn't heel, he trotted ahead, but always he looked back and kept a watchful eye on Ricky. When Bones was eager and excited, as he was now, he carried his tail high, curled up like a spring over his back.

They took the familiar path up to the school and went beyond it to the trailhead. They crossed the little wooden bridge over Bear Creek. Ricky looked to see if there were any new tracks, and he was rewarded. "Look!" he said to Bones. "Wild turkey tracks!" He pulled out his smart phone and took a picture. Then he reached in his pocket, took out a quarter, and put it near the track and took another picture. This way, he'd have a size reference. He could tell the track was about three-and-a half inches tall and a little wider than that.

Instead of taking the trail up Mole Hill, Ricky led them to the left along the edge of the hill and into a narrow canyon. Soon they reached a trail marker that Ricky stopped to read.

"Here we are, Bones. This is where the Bear Mountain Trail begins. Look up there!" Ricky pointed up the mountain. "That's where we're headed." Bones cocked his head and listened, but instead of looking up the mountain, he looked straight at Ricky.

The trail was steep, and they climbed without stopping for almost two hours. Although it was only mid-morning, it was already getting warm. Ricky had worn a long-sleeved shirt over his tee-shirt. When they paused beneath the shade of a pine tree, Ricky pulled off his pack, took off his shirt, and stuffed it inside.

"Time for a rest, Bones," Ricky said. He dropped to the ground, and Bones flopped down beside him. Ricky poured himself and his dog a drink. Then Ricky munched on his power bar and gave Bones one of his doggie treats.

"Come on," Ricky said, after about five minutes. He stood and pulled on his pack. "We've got another hour to go." They set off up the steep rocky trail until they finally reached the top of Bear Peak and a great viewpoint.

Ricky picked out a shady spot beneath a pine tree and leaned back against a rock. Bones sat down too, panting. Both of them had a drink and sat there for a few minutes, catching their breath.

While they rested, Ricky unsnapped Bones from his leash. Leash laws or no leash laws, he knew Bones wanted to do some exploring. "There's no one around," he said. "So you won't bother anyone, but stay close." Bones began nosing about the area.

When Ricky said, "Time for lunch," Bones bounded over. Ricky gave him a doggie treat before biting into one of his peanut butter and jelly sandwiches. He followed this with another drink and a couple of Oreos.

While he ate, Ricky took time to look down at Boulder. It was a great view from up here. He could pick out Viele Lake and the campus of the University, and he could see straight-as-an arrow Baseline Road heading east. Ricky pulled out his second sandwich and ate half of it while Bones watched anxiously, occasionally running a tongue over his nose and giving a little whimper.

"You know this last part's for you, don't you?" Ricky said. "But I'm going to give it to you piece by piece or it'll be gone in one gulp."

Ricky pulled off a piece of the sandwich and handed it to Bones. As always, Bones took it delicately from Ricky's hand. He downed it quickly and thumped his tail. Ricky fed the sandwich in quarters to Bones who beat the ground with his tail after every bite.

Lunch was good, the view was great, and Ricky was in no hurry to head back down. Instead he lay on his back, yawned contentedly, and looked up at the big clouds starting to build up. These were thunderheads, and he knew that there would likely be another lightning storm this afternoon. Summer storms usually came about three o'clock, but he planned to be home well before then.

As Ricky lay back, Bones explored. Something in the dry grass caught his attention. He sniffed and then wildly began barking.

"What have you found, Bones?" Ricky asked. He got to his feet and walked over. There was a pile of scat and a pungent odor. "Hey, that looks like bear droppings. Ricky uneasily gave a quick look around. "I guess there's a reason why they called this place Bear Mountain. Maybe we'd..." Before Ricky finished his sentence, Bones gave a sudden bark and bounded into the nearby shrubbery.

"Oh, no!" Ricky shouted. "Bones! Get back here!" Ricky could tell that Bones had found something. Bones barked frantically. It wasn't a bear. It was something small, black and white.

Peeeyew! An awful smell filled the air. Something like burning rubber.

"Bones, come here! Right now." Bones obeyed, but it was too late.

"Ugh! Skunk!" Ricky said, holding his nose and scrambling back to the tree.

Bones followed him. He put his head down and rubbed a paw across his eyes as he whined. Bones knew something was terribly wrong.

Ricky examined his dog to see if he was cut or scratched. He wasn't, but Bones had been badly skunked. The spray reeked. Ricky's eyes smarted and watered.

"Bad dog, Bones," Ricky said. "We are never going to hear the end of this."

CHAPTER 7

Ricky packed up in seconds, snapped on the leash, and hurriedly started back down the trail. "We've got to get you home as quick as we can and de-skunk you," he said.

They walked as fast as they could, and fortunately didn't meet anyone on the smelly hike home. As they walked, Ricky had plenty of time to make a plan of action. When they arrived, Ricky took Bones directly through the back fence gate into the backyard. He dropped his pack there, too. Ricky was afraid that he smelled as bad as Bones at this point.

Ricky hurried back out the gate and quietly entered the house through the garage. Meeting no one, he hurried to the bathroom and leaped into the shower. He scrubbed his body and his hair. When he got out, he tossed his smelly clothes onto the shower floor and left the water running. They'd get a quick rinse this way. Wrapped in a towel, he ran to his room and pulled on clean old clothes.

Ricky came back to the bathroom and turned off the water, leaving his wet clothes on the shower floor. As he hurried downstairs, Ricky offered a short prayer that Annabelle would be out. He was lucky. Only his mother and Mike were in the family room. Both were grading school papers.

"Hi," his mom said, catching sight of him. "I heard you come in. You hit the shower fast. Was it that hot up there on the mountain?"

"Worse than that," Ricky said. "Bones got skunked."

"What do you mean?" Mom asked, dropping the papers in her hand.

"He got sprayed," Ricky said. "By a skunk. You wouldn't believe the stink!"

"Where is he?" Mike asked, getting up from his chair.

"Out in the backyard," Ricky said.

All three of them went out into the backyard and Bones came bounding up.

"Sit," Ricky ordered while Bones was still some feet away. Bones stopped where he was and sat. But he was close enough for Mom and Mike to both hold their noses.

"Let's retreat," Mom said, and led the three of them back into the house.

"What do we do?" Ricky asked.

"I think I've heard some old remedy about bathing the dog in tomato juice," Ricky's mother said, "but I have doubts about that."

"Well, some sort of bath is definitely in order, and the quicker the better," Mike said.

"I'll bet the Internet would have something about it." Ricky went pounding up the stairs to his room. He sat in front of his computer and typed in, 'Skunk smell dog,' hoping for the best. That did it.

He quickly found several sites. All seemed to agree on the best concoction to de-skunk a dog, including one site that was advice from a vet. Ricky printed out the recipe and ran back downstairs.

"We need three percent hydrogen peroxide, baking soda, liquid dish soap, a scrubbing brush, and a bucket," he announced.

"I'll round up the stuff," Mom said, "and some rubber gloves."

Mike went to get a bucket.

When all was assembled, Ricky mixed the ingredients in the bucket and added a cup of water. The mixture began to bubble like some sort of witches' brew.

"You two don't have to go out and get all smelly. I'll give him the bath," Ricky said. "And I'll be careful. The Internet articles all said not to let any of the peroxide get in his eyes."

"I think you'll need help," Mike said.

"Help with what?" Annabelle asked, as she came walking into the house. She sniffed. "And what is that awful smell?"

Ricky ignored Annabelle and turned to Mike. "No, thanks," Ricky said. "I can do it, and there's no point in everyone getting wet. Just open the door for me, please."

His mother held open the door while Ricky carried the bucket and scrubbing brush outside. Ricky heard Mike start to explain what was going on to Annabelle. Before his mother shut the sliding door, Ricky could hear Annabelle break into wild giggles. He knew it would be a long time before he heard the end of this.

Ricky turned on the garden hose and let it run into the lawn. He set the bucket down on the edge of the patio. "Come here, Bones," he called. Obediently, Bones came over and looked suspiciously at the bucket. "Now stay still while I try to de-skunk you."

Bones didn't like baths, and he wasn't much for standing still, but he did seem to realize that there was something terribly wrong with him. There was a lot of wiggling and struggling, But Ricky hung on and Bones took it all pretty well. Fortunately, it was hot, so it didn't really matter that, with all the splashing going on, Ricky was soon as wet as Bones.

Ricky was gentle with the dog's face and careful to keep the solution away from Bones' eyes. He scrubbed hard on the rest of him. He tried to concentrate completely on what he was doing and not think about having to face Annabelle.

Ricky's mother opened the sliding door long enough to throw out several old towels. "Use these," she said, before quickly closing the door again.

After a thorough bath, Ricky picked up the garden hose and gave Bones a good rinse.

At this point, Mike and Ricky's mother, who'd been watching through the patio door, came out. They both sniffed.

"Better," his mother said. "Much better, but not gone."

"Definitely not all gone," Mike agreed.

"I'm afraid a second bath is in order," Mom said.

Ricky toweled himself off a bit, came back in, and began mixing up another de-skunking shampoo.

Annabelle made an elaborate show of holding her nose the minute he stepped inside, but didn't say a word. Ricky caught Mike giving her a stern look, and he was pretty sure Annabelle had been threatened to keep still. Ricky made a point of not looking at her.

Once more, Ricky mixed the shampoo ingredients in the bucket and went back outside. Bones wasn't thrilled, but he behaved reasonably. After another scrubbing, Ricky again took the hose and rinsed off his dog. Then Ricky took the old towels and dried Bones off.

Again Mike and Ricky's mother came out, sniffing the air.

"I think that second bath did it," Ricky's mother said. "Now, you go take another shower, Ricky. Be sure to shampoo your hair. I'll gather up all your clothes and wash them."

"Leave Bones out here for a while," Mike suggested. "He can dry off and air off, too."

Ricky took his time in the shower. He knew that he'd have to come out sometime, and when he did, he'd have to admit that he'd let Bones off his leash. Worst of all, he'd have to face Annabelle, too.

The moment after he left the shower, wrapped in a fresh towel, and stepped into his bedroom and shut the door, Ricky heard his mother gathering clothes and starting to clean the bathroom.

And he heard Annabelle say, "Let's open the window wide. I'll spray some lavender air freshener in here. That may help a little."

"Ugh," Ricky thought. He'd have to admit that lavender wasn't as bad as eau de skunk, but he hated the air fresheners Annabelle was constantly spraying in the bathroom. As soon as he was dressed, Ricky went back downstairs and joined everyone in the family room.

"Tell us what happened," his mother said.

Ricky told them about his hike, including the fact that he'd taken off the leash while they ate lunch.

"Boulder's Open Space leash laws are meant to keep dogs from bothering other hikers and dogs and from chasing deer," Mike said. "Now we know there's another good reason."

"I won't take him off leash again," Ricky promised.

"I'm glad that you met up with a skunk instead of something worse," Ricky's mother said. "If I'd had time to read the paper this morning before you and Bones left, you wouldn't have been up there on that trail. When I finally got around to reading it, I saw an article about a mountain lion spotted at the south end of town. A man, out after dark, said he saw a mountain lion catching a Canada goose down at Viele Lake. That's only about six blocks away. No more hiking for you and Bones in the hills until we know what's happening with that cougar."

Losing his freedom to go hiking was a blow to Ricky, but he was not in any position to argue about it.

The phone rang, and Ricky's mother answered it and then brought the phone to Ricky.

"It's Jose," she said.

"*Hola,*" Ricky said as he happily took the phone. He continued his conversation in Spanish, laughing now and again. Finally he hung up.

Annabelle looked at him in irritation. "It's not polite to talk in code," she said.

"Code? I was speaking in Spanish," Ricky replied angrily. "And it's not polite to listen in on others' conversations," he added.

"I wasn't trying to listen in. It's just your gibberish is annoying." Annabelle said.

"Jose is a boy visiting his grandmother who is one of our oldest neighbors in Broomfield," Ricky's mother explained. "He doesn't speak much English yet.

"But Spanish is not gibberish, Annabelle," she went on. "It's really a pretty language. You may decide to study it when you go to middle school next year. It's offered along with French and German."

While they were talking, the sky began to darken. "We're about to get another thunderstorm," Mike observed.

"Mom, can I have another old towel to get Bones really dry so he can come in?" Ricky asked. "You know if it starts to thunder, he'll go bananas out there."

Ricky took another old towel that his mother gave him and went back out to briskly rub down his dog. Either Ricky's nose was no longer working well, or the second bath really had done the job. Ricky thought that Bones smelled a little of wet dog, but he couldn't smell the skunk any more.

They hurried inside as the first raindrops began to fall. A streak of lightning flashed across the sky, followed by a loud rumble.

"Oooh, don't let that smelly dog near us," Annabelle said the moment Ricky entered the house. "Keep him away from Darwin and me." She picked up her cat and carried it into the living room.

Ricky bit his tongue. He wanted to say, *Believe me, the farther Bones and me are from you and that cat, the happier we'll be.* But he didn't want to start a war. Instead, he said, "I'll keep him in my room." Annabelle always made him feel unimportant, not good enough to be in her house.

There was another boom of thunder. The foolish dog that wasn't afraid of bears or skunks ran for the stairs. Ricky knew that Bones would take refuge under the bed, and once again, he half-wished he could join him.

CHAPTER 8

At lunch on Monday, Ricky had no sooner settled down at a cafeteria table with George, Wally, and Yan than Annabelle and two of her friends appeared. They went out of their way to walk next to the boys' table. Each of the three girls balanced her lunch tray on one hand and held her nose with the other hand, making gasping noises as they slowly paraded by. Naturally, heads turned to stare.

Ricky felt himself grow hot, but he said nothing. He hadn't mentioned the skunk episode to his friends.

"What's that about?" Wally asked, as he watched the girls go by.

Ricky's first impulse was to pretend ignorance, but he thought better of it. The truth would no doubt come out. The skunk episode was a good story, and Annabelle was going to spread it everywhere she could. Ricky decided he'd best fess up and put the whole thing in a humorous light.

Ricky told about the skunking and the major clean up afterwards. He laughed at himself and was careful to put the emphasis on the bubbly witches' brew he'd concocted to get rid of the smell. "You can find a recipe for anything on the Net," he said.

Wally, Yan, and George had a good laugh, and that was the end of it.

"Have you guys thought at all about your careers report?" George asked.

"No," Ricky admitted. "How about you? Do you know what you want to be some day?"

"I wouldn't mind being a star in a big rock band," George said. "But I'll probably do something with computers."

Wally said, "I plan to be a great chef one day. How about you, Ricky?"

"I don't know what I'd like to do," Ricky said. "I know I don't want to be a teacher. Maybe something with animals. Work in a zoo or a fish hatchery, or something."

That afternoon during class meeting time, the two fifth grades voted on what they wanted to do for Friday's entertainment at Camp Betasso. Their choices were a Sing Along, proposed by Mr. Bennett's class, or the Magic Show which Ricky had suggested. Ricky's class unanimously voted for the Magic Show. Mid-period, Mrs. Hannigan and Mr. Bennett exchanged notes, and it was revealed that two-thirds of Mr. Bennett's class had voted for the Magic Show, too.

George and Wally leaned over to thump Ricky on the back. Ricky felt very good that his idea had won out, and he was confident that everyone would enjoy Marko the Magnificent. He wasn't so sure how good his own magic trick would be. He was pretty rusty. He'd have to squeeze in some practice this week.

As soon as he got home from school, Ricky told his mother

about the fifth graders choosing the Magic Night for entertainment, and she called up Marko to share the news.

At the dinner table that night, Annabelle talked about the Outdoor Ed again. "I don't know what's wrong with the kids in my class," she complained. "They voted to have a dumb old magic show for Friday night entertainment."

Ricky saw his mother glance at him in surprise.

"I wanted to have a Sing Along," Annabelle continued. "I was going to make sure that the music teacher put the words to Miley Cyrus's song, *Butterfly, Fly Away,* on the song sheet. All of us in the Butterfly Cabin know that song."

"Too bad," Ricky said. The he added as casually as he could, "The magic show was my idea, and I think it's going to be a lot of fun."

"Your idea?" Annabelle was clearly shocked. It actually shut her up for a minute.

Ricky thought with satisfaction that Annabelle hadn't dreamed he would offer an idea that would be selected.

"Yeah," Ricky went on. "Marko the Magnificent performs at lots of parties in Broomfield, and Mom and I know him. Mom called him up, and he said he'd be glad to come and perform for free. He's really good."

Annabelle looked from Ricky to her stepmother in surprise.

Ricky's mother hastened to say, "I called Marko this afternoon, and he's looking forward to it. But there'll probably be other times at camp for singing."

Annabelle had little to say during the remainder of dinner.

Ricky went to bed, feeling pretty good. The skunk issue was pretty much behind him. Oh, he'd probably get a few more stink-o comments, but he could handle that. And because he'd suggested bringing Marko the Magnificent to Camp Betasso, kids in the class seemed to know his name now. Things were definitely looking better.

Ricky was sound asleep at three in the morning when he was awakened by frantic barking. He struggled to come fully awake and sat up in bed and listened. Sure enough, Bones was making a huge ruckus.

Ricky swung his legs over the bed and stood up. All this time, the wild barking continued. Something was really wrong. Bones never carried on like that. Ricky didn't bother to pull on a robe or slippers; he just started down the stairs.

"Will somebody shut that mutt up?" came a loud wail from Annabelle's room.

Ricky quickened his pace. When he was halfway down the stairs, he heard the door open to his mother and Mike's bedroom. Glancing up, he saw Mike, tying his bathrobe, and also heading down the stairs.

When they entered the kitchen, Ricky and Mike found Bones crouched and barking fiercely through the cat door.

"Hey! Bones!" Ricky said. "What's gotten into you? Be quiet!"

Bones ignored him, and his barking increased.

"There's got to be something outside that's really bothering Bones," Mike said. He looked out into the darkness through the sliding door. Then he switched on the patio light. There was nothing unusual on the cement patio just outside the door, but the patio light didn't illuminate the far corner of the yard or the shrubbery areas along the fence. Mike and Ricky stared outside.

Finally Mike cracked open the door just a little and listened. "What's that?" he asked.

Bones was barking even louder, but through the cracked open

door another sound could be heard, the yowling of a cat.

"Darwin?" Mike asked. He and Ricky quickly looked around the family room for some sign of the cat. Darwin wasn't dozing on his favorite cushion on the bench seat in front of the fireplace. In fact, Darwin was nowhere to be seen.

Mike slid the door wide open. Clearly this was the moment that Bones had been waiting for. He rushed through the door, almost knocking Mike off balance as he went. Without hesitation, Bones raced for the far corner of the yard, barking furiously as he went.

At this point, Ricky's mother and Annabelle both came trailing downstairs to see what all the racket was about. Ricky started through the open door after Bones.

"Wait, Ricky!" Mike said. "We don't know what's going on out there."

Mike hurried over to the kitchen sink where he always kept an emergency flashlight. He picked it up and stepped just outside the door. Ricky followed and stood beside him. Advancing slowly, Mike aimed his light into the far corner of the yard.

"Bones!" Ricky yelled into the darkness. "Bones! Get back here."

Slowly they walked to the edge of the patio, peering back into the far corner of the yard. Ricky gasped. Two gleaming eyes of a large animal stared at him.

With his heart in his throat, Ricky realized he was looking at a mountain lion.

CHAPTER 9

"Get back in the house. Quick!" Mike ordered, and he grabbed Ricky's arm, pulling him. They backed away toward the door.

Ricky's mom slid it open. "Is that a mountain lion?" she asked, staring out the sliding door. Her voice shook.

"Yeah!" Ricky yelled. "What'll we do?"

Ricky's mother gasped and grabbed them both tightly for a moment. Then she leaped into action. "Noise! Loud noises will scare it away!"

Ricky's mom ran to the kitchen, grabbed whatever pots and pans she could, jerked open the drawer, picked up a handful of spoons, and thrust them at the others. They all stood in front of the sliding door in the family room, beating on the pots and pans, making a horrible din.

"And yell," Ricky said, beating on a pan and shouting at the top of his lungs, "Get away. Get away from here."

The lights, barking dog, pots, pans and screams must have been too much for the mountain lion. As Ricky watched from inside the sliding glass door, he saw the cougar give one graceful and powerful leap that allowed him to clear the wooden grape stake fence and disappear on the other side.

Immediately, Ricky slid open the sliding door, but Mike put his arm on Ricky's shoulder and stopped him from going outside. "Wait!" he said. "It isn't safe out there."

While he stood staring out the door, worried about Bones, Ricky noticed the lights coming on next door in the neighbor's house.

Ricky's mother ran to the phone. She called the police to report what was happening. A moment later, she said, "The police are on their way, and they're sending someone from Colorado Parks and Wildlife. Now I'm going to call Paul, next door. I don't want anyone in his family stepping out into the yard. That cougar may still be there." She quickly punched in the number on her cell phone.

Ricky's heart was pounding. He had to get his dog back. "Bones!" he yelled. "Bones, come here." Mike still gripped Ricky's shoulder, so he remained inside, but he slid open the patio door.

Bones had raced over to the spot where the mountain lion cleared the fence, but after a few more barks, he came running to Ricky.

As soon as Bones was inside, Ricky threw his arms around Bones and hugged him. "Good, boy," Ricky said. "You're a hero." He examined the dog and was relieved to see that Bones didn't even have a scratch. "Crazy dog," Ricky said, giving him another hug.

The moment Ricky released his hold on Bones, the dog raced

back to the door which was only open a crack, and frantically scratched at it. Through the door from the far corner of the yard, came a pitiful yowling.

"Darwin?" Annabelle said. "Is that Darwin out there?" She ran to the door.

Mike stopped her. "You wait inside, honey," Mike said. "It's not safe out."

Ricky's mother had finished talking to the neighbor, and she put one arm around Annabelle and the other around Ricky as they all crowded around the door.

Mike slid open the door and stepped outside, carrying the flashlight with him. Bones leaped through the open door and raced toward the wailing that was coming from the yard. It was so dark back there that Ricky couldn't see what Mike was doing, but they watched him kneel down and pick up something. He hurried back toward the house, and Bones, whining a little, trotted right beside him.

"Maria, get some towels," Mike yelled as he approached the door.

While Ricky's mom ran to get towels, Mike reached the door. In his arms, he carried Darwin, whose black fur was matted with blood.

"Darwin!" Annabelle screamed. She reached out for her cat. The cat jerked and meowed.

"Sit down and hold him gently," Ricky's mom said. She spread out a towel on Annabelle's lap. "Try to keep him warm and quiet. We'll take him to the vet as soon as we can."

Annabelle sat on the couch, holding Darwin gently and crooning to him. Ricky sat across the room petting Bones.

Someone pounded on the door. Mike ran and looked out the

front window where he could see the police had arrived. Another car was pulling up. It must be one from Parks and Wildlife. Mike opened the door and talked to the visitors. Ricky's mother ran upstairs and pulled on some clothes. Then she came back downstairs, made another hurried phone call, and went into the family room.

She gently took Darwin onto her lap. One ear was badly torn, and there was a lot of blood on the cat's stomach. Ricky looked at the cat and then he looked at Annabelle, who was very pale and biting her lip. He gave Bones another hug.

"While Darwin and I wait here, you two run upstairs and get dressed," Ricky's mom said. "I called the all-night vet emergency room, and they're expecting Darwin as soon as we can get him there."

Ricky and Annabelle raced upstairs. For once, Annabelle beat Ricky in getting dressed and back down to the family room. She got a small throw blanket from the couch and wrapped Darwin, towels and all, into a bundle.

While Ricky's mom went and talked to Mike, Ricky took Bones upstairs to his bedroom. "I'm not letting you out in the yard again tonight, boy," Ricky said to his dog. "So you just stay in here and keep quiet until I get back. You hear?"

Bones wagged his tail.

Before he left his bedroom, Ricky dropped down to one knee and took his dog's head into his hands and looked right into his eyes. "You were brave, Bones, to help Darwin like that. I'm proud of you. But that's it. No more mixing it up with a skunks, bears, or mountain lions. You hear me?" Bones thumped his tail. "I couldn't get along without you, boy."

Ricky slipped out of the room, pulling on his jacket as he went. He hurried down to the car. Annabelle was already sitting in the backseat with Darwin in her arms. She sat silently, but tears were running down her cheeks. Ricky hesitated for a minute. Should he sit in back with Annabelle, or not? He opened the door to the front seat and climbed in. Only a minute later, Ricky's mom came out of the house into the garage. Hurriedly she climbed in, opened the garage door, and drove off.

"We're not going to your regular vet, Annabelle, but to a pet hospital that's open all night for emergencies. It's not far, and we'll be there in a few minutes."

"Hurry," Annabelle choked out. "Please, please hurry!"

CHAPTER 10

At the clinic, things happened fast. Ricky's mom rang the emergency bell while Annabelle hugged Darwin in his blankets and towels close to her chest. A middle-aged man quickly opened the door and let them in. He led the way behind the counter and down a short hall to an examination room.

"Please put your cat on the table," he said to Annabelle. "Darwin, isn't it?"

She nodded.

"Hold him gently while I scrub up." The doctor washed up thoroughly and put on his gloves.

Ricky was impressed that the vet knew and remembered the cat's name from the one short and hurried call his mother had made.

"You folks can wait here, if you want, or out in the waiting room."

"Here," Annabelle said quickly.

Ricky's mother took Annabelle's hand and moved her back a short distance from the table.

The doctor unwrapped Darwin, who gave a faint meow. The vet took a quick look, and then leaned over to the counter, picked up a syringe that was ready, and gave Darwin an injection.

"This will put Darwin to sleep so he won't be uncomfortable while I work on him," the vet said. Each step of the way, as the doctor worked, he explained what he was doing. He cleaned Darwin, shaved a little of the stomach fur, carefully examined the wound and stitched it closed.

Then he wrapped Darwin in a clean blanket and handed him to Annabelle. As she cradled the cat, Ricky saw the tears in her eyes.

"Come with me, and I'll show you where Darwin will spend the night." The vet led Annabelle through a door and into a small back room. Ricky and his mother followed them and watched Annabelle put Darwin onto a soft little bed of blankets.

When they came back out, the vet led them all back to the waiting room. He gave Ricky's mom a paper to fill out on a clipboard while he talked with them.

"Darwin should be fine," the vet said. "He's a very lucky cat. One ear is torn, and the mountain lion must have raked his claws across Darwin's stomach. But the wound isn't deep. That cougar must have been distracted in some way, because it could easily have killed Darwin." He turned to Ricky, "You say your dog ran out and surprised the mountain lion?"

"Yes, sir," Ricky said. He glanced proudly over at Annabelle. "He was a real hero. He knew Darwin was out there, and he went to protect him." Ricky waited for Annabelle to chime in and praise Bones, but she didn't say a word.

"And the dog wasn't hurt?"

"Not a scratch," Ricky replied.

"You're twice lucky then." The vet smiled. "Darwin is going to have to stay for several days," the doctor continued. "I hate to keep him, because cats really stress out when they aren't home in familiar surroundings. But he's weak, traumatized, and has lost blood. Most important, we have to be sure that no infection sets in. If all goes well, and I think it will, you should be able to take Darwin home this Saturday."

"But I don't want him to be here all alone," Annabelle said.

"I know, but he really needs our care," the vet said. "Mornings are especially busy here with surgeries and admissions, but you can phone any day in the afternoon, for a report, and maybe you can even visit."

"We'll call every day, Annabelle," Ricky's mom promised. "Thank you, doctor," she said. She gave him the forms she had completed and shook hands with him.

Ricky's mom led the way back to the car, and everyone climbed in.

The moment they reached home and the car was parked in the garage, Annabelle jumped out. She ran inside to her father and sobbed. Ricky and his mother followed. When Annabelle was quiet, she told her father all about the visit to the vet, and the good news that Darwin would be well enough to come home by the weekend.

"The vet was wonderful," Annabelle said.

While Annabelle told her father the story, Ricky slipped upstairs and let Bones out of the bedroom. Bones happily came back downstairs, and Ricky gave him a doggy treat. Ricky's mom made some hot chocolate for everyone, and they all sat at the kitchen table. It was Mike's turn to fill everyone in on what had happened while they were gone.

"The police took my report and two people arrived from

Colorado Parks and Wildlife, a Division Wildlife Manager and his assistant. They talked with our neighbor, too. They brought two tracking dogs with them. The men seemed sure the cougar would go back up toward Mesa School and onto the Open Space land up there."

"What are they going to do?" Ricky asked.

"They'll try to track the mountain lion down," Mike said. "Hopefully, they'll find it. They have guns and tranquilizing darts. They'll tranquilize it, and while it's asleep, they'll tag it, put it a cage, and take it far away from here and release it in the wild."

"Why do they tag it?" Ricky asked.

"They try to give the animal a chance," Mike explained. "They hope that if they take it a couple of hundred miles away and release it in in the wild, it will stay there. But if it comes back to town where it's a threat to livestock, pets, and people, and they're called out again, they'll see the tag and know it's the same cat. Then they might be forced to kill it."

"Now that's sounds like exciting work," Ricky said. "Maybe I'll write my careers report about a Wildlife Manager."

"One of the men who came here gave me his card," Mike said. "I'm sure if you called him he could tell you more about it."

"I'm sure glad that lion is going to be far, far away," Ricky added, "but I hope they don't have to kill it."

"That's because it didn't tear up your dumb dog," Annabelle shouted. "I'd like to kill it. It almost killed Darwin." While she spoke, Annabelle glared at Bones who was sitting at Ricky's feet.

"Well, my dog probably saved your cat," Ricky said. How could Annabelle be so ungrateful? "You might even thank him."

"Thank him? He's the cause of all this."

"What do you mean?" Ricky asked.

"Why do you think that cougar came to our yard? Do you think we were just 'lucky?' No.

"That mountain lion came because your dog was dumb enough to tangle with a skunk last weekend. That skunk smell is still everywhere, and I'm sure that's why the mountain lion came!"

Everyone was quiet during this outburst. Ricky stared at Annabelle in disbelief. He was furious. Not only was Annabelle not going to thank Bones for braving a mountain lion and saving Darwin's life, she was going to blame him for the attack.

CHAPTER 11

"Honey," Mike said, looking at Annabelle, and reaching across the table to take her hand. "This has been a terrible night. Just awful. I know how worried you are about Darwin. We've all been scared half out of our wits. But you can't blame this on Bones. It isn't fair."

"Fair? Who cares about fair?" Annabelle blurted out. "If it weren't for Bones and his stinky skunk smell, Darwin wouldn't be sleeping tonight at the vet's with his stomach torn open and his ear half gone."

There was a moment of complete silence in the room.

Then Ricky, eyes blazing, pushed back his chair and stood. He glared straight at Annabelle. "You're right about one thing. Without Bones, your cat *wouldn't* be sleeping at the vet's. Darwin would be dead. Bones is the one who sounded the alarm and woke us up. Bones is the one that rushed out and faced the mountain lion and scared him off. Bones is a hero, and you ought to be thanking him!" Ricky took a couple of steps over to Bones, dropped down on his knees, and pulled Bones close to him.

Ricky's mother came over and knelt beside Ricky. "Mike's right. We're all exhausted and none of us is thinking straight." She gave Ricky a hug and got to her feet, glancing at the clock. "It's almost five o'clock! Mike and I have got to go to school and teach in a couple of hours. I think you kids need to just sleep in this morning." She glanced at Mike, and he nodded. "I'll call the school a little later and excuse you both. You can go up to class this afternoon after you've rested if you feel like it, or you can take the whole day off."

"Good idea," Mike agreed. "After breakfast, I'll phone Mrs. Schumacher and ask her to look in on you at noon time to see if you need anything."

Ricky looked at Annabelle, waiting for her to say something. Apologize, admit how awful she'd been. But nothing. Ricky got up and headed for the stairs. "Come on, Bones."

When he got to his room, Ricky closed the bedroom door, pulled off his jeans, and fell into bed. Only minutes later, he heard his mother come in, but he didn't stir or open his eyes, and she quietly tip-toed out again.

Ricky lay there with his fists clenched for a while. Gradually, he relaxed a little. Skipping a day of school while not even being sick might have been tempting under some circumstances. But Ricky had no desire to be under the same roof with Annabelle. He was still seething. He was also exhausted, and somehow he fell asleep.

Ricky's internal clock woke him at quarter of seven just as if there hadn't been three hours of rest ripped right out of the middle of his usual night's sleep. He quickly dressed and luxuriated in having the bathroom to himself. That was a first! There were no sounds coming from Annabelle's room. Ricky didn't slam about, but he made no particular effort to be quiet, either. He didn't care if Annabelle slept or woke or disappeared into thin air.

When Ricky came downstairs, with Bones trailing him, he found his Mom and Mike talking quietly. Both of them looked pretty tired and droopy.

"Hey! What are you doing up?" Mike asked.

"Aren't you awfully tired?" his mom asked, as she stood up and gave him a hug. "I thought you'd be staying home this morning."

Ricky let Bones outside. "No," he said, "I don't feel especially tired. I'd rather go to school than sit around all morning."

Ricky walked over to the counter and began to fix some toast. He popped in two pieces of bread and then took out the butter and jelly.

No one seemed to have anything more to say. Finally, Mike broke the silence. "I'm sorry that Annabelle accused Bones of being the cause of the mountain lion's visit."

Ricky looked up from the toaster. "No need for *you* to be sorry," Ricky said. "Annabelle's the one who should be sorry and apologize to Bones."

"And I'm sure she will," Ricky's mother added. "I know things will look a lot different to her when she wakes up today. Last night she wasn't herself."

Ricky kept his mouth closed tightly but he thought, *Oh, yes she was. She was her usual self-centered self.* As Ricky looked out into the backyard, he watched Bones rushing about, sniffing here and there, and finally standing on his hind legs and pawing the fence at the spot where the mountain lion had leaped over.

Breakfast was a hurried and quiet affair. Ricky's mother and Mike drove away at their usual times, and Ricky walked out the back door soon after. He took his smartphone with him and headed for the far corner. In the damp soil, he found some great cougar prints. Ricky took several pictures, including one with his quarter to have a size comparison.

The cougar print was about three inches high and four inches wide. The four toe pads showed distinctly, as did the large foot pad. The cougar's retractable claws didn't show in the track.

Ricky took a moment to say good-bye to Bones and even gave him a doggy treat. He left Bones out in the yard and glared at the cat door as he left. Mike still hadn't touched it.

CHAPTER 12

Ricky hadn't gone more than four houses up the street when he heard a voice calling out behind him.

"Hey, Ricky! Wait up!"

Ricky turned and saw George running up behind him.

"Geez," George said. "There must have been a lot of excitement around here last night, and I slept through it. Mike called my mom this morning and told her all about it. Mom's going over to your place at lunchtime to check on Annabelle." He gazed at Ricky wide-eyed. "Did you really have a mountain lion in your backyard?"

"Yeah," Ricky said. He stopped and pulled out his phone. "Here's its footprint." George stared wide-eyed at the picture of the track.

As they fell into step together and headed toward school, Ricky told George all about what had happened. As he spoke, Ricky got caught up in the adventure and at least for the moment forgot all about Annabelle. News spread at school, and Ricky found himself re-telling the same story to each eager new group. Mrs. Hannigan must have heard the tale during morning recess, because when they came back in, she had Ricky tell the story to the whole class and show the pictures of the tracks.

Ricky was suddenly famous. Instead of the "new kid," he was now the "lion kid." He still might not know many of the students in this new school, but now they all knew him. Ricky wondered if Annabelle might show up at school during the noon hour, but if she did, he didn't see her.

During a library period, Ricky took some time to look up Division Wildlife Managers on one of the computers. He really did think that might be a great career. In addition to college, he learned it required additional time studying about police work and wildlife management. One of the articles pointed out that as towns grew and people built houses in mountain areas, there were more and more instances of wild animals and people confronting one another.

During the last hour of the day, at class meeting time, there was more discussion about Outdoor Education at Camp Betasso.

"Remember," Mrs. Hannigan said, "that anyone can sign up to perform in the magic show. Students will present their acts before Marko the Magnificent performs. I've taped a sign-up sheet here on the inside of the door," she pointed, "and you just have to be sure you sign up by Thursday afternoon."

Ricky glanced over at Yan, who was puffing out his chest and pointing at himself.

When the dismissal bell rang, Yan came over to join Wally, George, and Ricky. "Who's going to perform magic?" he asked.

"Not me," Wally said.

"Me, neither," said George.

"Guess it's you and me, man," Yan said, punching Ricky lightly on the shoulder. "Let's sign up now."

After the boys signed the sheet, they all headed out the door together. Once on the sidewalk, Wally called goodbye and headed off in the opposite direction as the other three started down the hill. Yan lived about a block east and two blocks north of Ricky and George. It was hot and muggy out, but there were no big thunderheads in the sky. Ricky gave a little sigh of relief. No thunder to worry about today. Poor old Bones had been through enough.

"We should practice our magic tricks," Yan said.

"I'm not going to do any tricks, but if either of you guys needs an assistant, I'll help," George volunteered.

"Thanks, but I don't need an assistant. All I need is a quarter, a glass, and a piece of newspaper," Yan said.

"I don't need an assistant, either," Ricky said. "What I need is an impresario."

"An impresario?" George said. "What's that?"

"Someone to introduce me properly. You know." Ricky suddenly switched to using a deep, booming, impressive voice. "Ladeeeez and gentlemen. Let me introduce to you Ricky the Remarkable, the Razzle-Dazzle Magician, who will absolutely amaze you!"

They all started to laugh.

"That's a great idea!" Yan said. "George, you can introduce both of us--Yan, Mighty Master of the Dark Arts and Ricky the Ridiculous!" Yan poked Ricky in the arm as he said this.

"Okay," George agreed. "I get it. I'll introduce you both and give you a big build-up."

Ricky breathed a sigh of relief, and he suspected Yan did too. If there was one thing Ricky hated to do, it was to speak in public. This way he and Yan could do the tricks and good old George would do most of the talking. Perfect.

"Maybe we can practice tonight after dinner," Yan suggested.

"Sure," Ricky said. "Good idea. Why don't you both come over to my house about seven o'clock? Yan and I will practice our magic, and you can practice your introduction, George, and be the audience, too. You can watch really close, and if we can fool you, we can fool the class."

They hurried the rest of the way home, promising to meet again soon. All Ricky had to worry about was keeping Annabelle out of their hair.

As soon as Ricky entered his house, he dropped his backpack and headed to the back yard to see Bones. Ricky couldn't help but notice Annabelle as he passed through the family room. Annabelle was listening to her music and curled up with a book. She didn't look up or speak, and that was fine with Ricky. He ignored her. As usual, as soon as he stepped outside, Ricky was welcomed with lots of tail wagging and a couple of slobbery kisses from Bones.

Ricky threw a ball for Bones to chase for a few minutes until he heard a car drive into the garage. This surprised him. Neither his mom nor Mike ever got home this early. Ricky whistled to Bones, and they both came inside to see what was going on.

"Hey, Ricky," Mike said. "I came home right after school today, because I promised Belle that I'd take her to the vet this afternoon so that she could see Darwin. Want to come with us?"

Ricky saw the daggered look that Annabelle shot at him. It was abundantly clear that she did not want his company.

"Thanks, but I'll stay here," Ricky said. "I've got some stuff I should be doing for school. If you have the card that Wildlife Manager left, I think I'll give him a call. I need to interview him for my careers report."

"Sure," Mike said. He went over to the counter, found the card and gave it to Ricky.

Ricky took the card and said, "Come on, Bones." Ricky picked up his backpack and headed up the stairs to his room with Bones bounding on ahead. "I hope Darwin's feeling a lot better today," Ricky called down.

There was no response from Annabelle.

Ricky really meant it. Darwin could be a bit of a pain, but he was a spunky little cat, and it wasn't his fault that he belonged to Annabelle. Ricky felt sorry for him.

As soon as he got upstairs, Ricky went in the room that served as a guest room and an office. He used the phone on the desk there and called up Ralph Owen, the Division Wildlife Manager. Ricky was surprised to catch him. Ricky explained who he was and how he was interested in writing a report about a career as a Division Wildlife Manager.

Mr. Owen said, "I have a packet of information I'll mail you, and I'd be glad to answer any questions that I can. You know my job isn't always as exciting as going out to hunt down a cougar." The officer laughed. "By the way, you'll want to know that we tracked your cougar and tranquilized him. Then we tagged him and took the cougar a couple hundred miles away, up into the mountains and released him. We hope we'll never see him down here again."

Ricky was glad to hear the report. "I'll pass that on," he said.

Officer Owen continued, "Your cougar was a healthy male, about seven or eight years old, I'd guess, and he weighed about 150 pounds. Instead of tracking cougars, much of my work time is checking hunting and fishing licenses, following up on poachers who shoot animals illegally, and visiting schools to talk about wildlife. What sort of things would you like to know?"

"What is a Division, anyway, and do you need to go to college be a Division Wildlife Manager?" Ricky asked.

"The state of Colorado is divided into over a hundred divisions," Mr. Owen said. "Each of us is responsible for an area. And yes, you need a college degree. You can major in a number of differ-ent fields for your Bachelor of Science Degree, in subjects like biol-ogy, zoology, forestry, or environmental science. And after college, it takes about another year of training."

"In what?" Ricky asked.

"Division Wildlife Managers are police officers," Mr. Owen ex-plained. "So they need to attend and pass training at a police acade-my. They learn about laws, regulations, firearms, how to interview people and even how to make an arrest and testify in court. And, of course, you have to pass a background check."

"Wow!" Ricky said.

"And then there's training in wildlife management. You must be able to drive a truck and even a snowmobile because you can be called out in all kinds of weather and terrain."

While Mr. Owen talked, Ricky scribbled notes as fast as he could.

"You need to be strong," Mr. Owen continued. "Able to lift fif-ty pounds. And you have to be a good team player, able to get along with your co-workers and with the public, too. You can read more about it in the packet I'm sending you. And feel free to call me any time. I'm not always around, but leave your number, and I'll get back to you. I'm glad you're interested."

Ricky said, "Thanks. You've been a big help."

Feeling good that he had made a start on his career report, Ricky went to his own room, switched on his favorite radio sta-tion, and quickly started his math homework. Since he was having friends over this evening, he knew the first thing his mother would ask was, "Is your homework done?" It didn't take long to solve the twelve problems. Math was his best subject.

That done, Ricky began to think about what he'd need for his magic trick. He'd already decided which one he'd like to do. He was pretty sure that many of the tricks done by the kids would involve coins or cards. Yan had said he'd be using a quarter. In some ways, these were the easiest. Of course, when you goofed up, you looked pretty silly, but that was the case with any magic trick.

Ricky wanted to do the Balloon Burst. It was different. All it took was a balloon, a needle, and a piece of sticky transparent tape. It was quick, and when it worked, it was pretty amazing. Getting to pop a balloon and make a big bang in front of a crowd was pretty fun, too.

Ricky ran back downstairs to get his supplies. In this new house, just like in their old place in Broomfield, Mom had quickly established what they called the "junk drawer." It was the place to look if you needed a balloon, a candle, a popsicle stick, a thumb tack, or something vital like a shoelace. Sure enough, tucked in among everything else in the drawer was a package of birthday balloons. Ricky chose three, one to use for practice tonight, one to use for the show, and a spare—just in case.

Then he went to the family room and took down the sewing box that was stored on a shelf there. Ricky's mom had taught him to sew on buttons, a skill she insisted that every man must have. Although sewing on a button was the full range of Ricky's sewing skills, at least he knew where to find a sharp needle when he needed it. And he needed one now.

Ricky took his stash of supplies up to his room, put them in a safe spot on the bookshelf, and then came back downstairs again. He was watching a TV show when his mom got home.

CHAPTER 13

"Hi," Maria called as she looked around. "Where is everybody?"

"Mike took Annabelle down to the vet to see Darwin," Ricky explained. "They should be back soon."

"I hope everything is all right," his mom said.

Ricky suspected that Darwin would be doing fine. But Annabelle? Who knew how the drama queen would be?

Without being asked, Ricky began to set the table as his mom started dinner preparations. She scrubbed up some potatoes and put them in the oven to bake while mixing chopped onion and breadcrumbs into ground meat that she shaped into a meat loaf.

"We never seem to have enchiladas or burritos anymore," Ricky observed.

"Annabelle isn't very fond of spicy food," his mother explained. She smiled at Ricky. "I'm hoping little by little she'll learn to like it."

Right, Ricky thought, not believing a word of it, *and she'll like mariachi music, too!*

"I asked George and Yan to come over tonight around seven o'clock," Ricky said. "Hope that's okay."

"Of course," his mother said. "If your homework's done."

"It is," Ricky said.

"What are you three going to be up to?"

"Yan and I signed up to do a magic trick at the Outdoor Ed camp. Any of the kids who want can do tricks that night before Marko the Magnificent performs."

"Hey! That sounds like fun," his mom said. "Have you picked out a trick?"

"Yeah, but while we practice tonight, can we have the basement room to ourselves?"

Ricky's mom stopped what she was doing to look him in the eye. "What you really mean is that you don't want Annabelle down there, right?"

Ricky squirmed a little. "Right," he admitted.

"That's not very friendly," she pointed out. "I don't think you need to worry. I'm sure Annabelle wouldn't want to go downstairs where you three boys were up to something. But you know that if you are going to perform magic up at Camp Betasso, you'll have to get used to performing in front of an audience."

"Yeah," Ricky said. "But while we practice and perfect our tricks, we need to do it in private. Magicians never give away their secrets."

It wasn't long before Mike and Annabelle got home. Annabelle rushed inside, crying, and without saying a word to anyone, ran up to her room and slammed the door.

"Oh, dear," Ricky's mother said. She put a hand to her heart.

Hesitantly, she turned to Mike and asked, "Darwin...is he ...?"

Mike came right to her and put his arms around her. "No, no. Darwin's doing fine. The vet says he'll be able to come home in a couple days."

Ricky and his mother both gave a little sigh of relief.

"Then why is Annabelle so upset?" Ricky's mother asked. "That's good news."

"Sure it is," Mike said. "We had a great visit. Annabelle had a million questions for the vet, and he was awfully good in spending time with her and showing her around the place. But Belle wanted to bring Darwin home NOW. She didn't want to leave him there another night. But that's doctor's orders."

"I got a call today," Ricky's mother said. "The Wildlife Manager reported that they tracked and tranquilized that mountain lion, and took him more than two hundred miles away to release."

"That's a relief," Mike said. "Let's hope he never visits our neighborhood again."

"I knew that," Ricky said. "And thanks for giving me Mr. Owen's business card. I phoned and talked with him this afternoon and he was helpful in my careers report."

Mike managed to coax Annabelle back downstairs for dinner. At first, she only picked at her food. Then she brightened and soon was her usual talkative self, sharing about her visit with the vet.

"I decided to write about a career as a veterinarian," she explained. "It's definitely not boring. Do you know that training to be a vet is a lot like training to be a doctor?"

"That makes sense," Ricky's mother said. "Vets deal with cuts and broken bones and diseases in pets just like doctors do in people."

"It's even more complicated," Annabelle said. "You have to

learn about all kinds of animals. All people have one stomach. Some animals have more than one. Some animals have front legs and some have flippers. You can work with big animals like horses and cows, or with wild animals in a zoo, or maybe a big aquarium. I think I'd like to work with pets, though. Did you know that Americans keep fifty-nine million cats as pets? More cats are pets than dogs," she added with a sniff in Ricky's direction.

She paused in her long speech to eat a few bites.

But before Ricky managed to say anything, Annabelle started in again.

"After college, where you should major in the sciences, you go on to a veterinary school. It's harder to get into than medical school! There are only thirty vet schools in the country, and one is real nearby, up in Fort Collins."

"Really?" Maria managed to get a word in.

"Yeah. And there are about two thousand new vets graduating from these schools every year. Then they have to take a test to practice in the state where they want to work. I took lots of notes for my career report," Annabelle added, giving a superior look to Ricky as she spoke.

"I started on my career report today, too," Ricky said. "I'm going to write about being a Division Wildlife Manager for the State of Colorado."

"I guess you don't need a lot of training to chase wild animals around at night," Annabelle observed.

"Just like a vet," Ricky said, happy to contradict her, "you go to college and major in one of the sciences. Then you take another year of training at a police academy and in wildlife management. It sounds tough, but really interesting."

"Sounds as if you both have special careers to explore," Mike said.

Ricky wanted to share more about what he'd learned about wildlife management, but he decided to wait for another time, and instead helped his mom clear the table and get the dishes into the dishwasher.

"You can pop this in the microwave for them," his mom suggested. She set out a package of popcorn, a bowl and some napkins.

"Thanks, Mom."

Ricky got his magic supplies from his room and set them on the counter. Then he put the bag of popcorn, correct side up, in the microwave and waited.

At seven o'clock, the doorbell rang. Ricky pushed the button on the microwave before he headed to the front door. Yan and George both came tumbling in. Yan carried a small paper sack.

"I'm making popcorn," Ricky said. "Then we'll go on down to the basement."

In just a couple of minutes, the three boys went pounding down the stairs, carrying the popcorn and their magic supplies. Bones followed them. All three boys sat on the old brown couch with Ricky in the middle, holding the bowl. Bones sat on the carpet in front of them and looked hopeful. Now and again, a boy would drop a kernel. Sometimes Ricky threw him a piece and Bones never missed catching it. After they'd made quick work of the popcorn, Ricky set up a card table and put a chair beside it.

"You go first, Yan."

Yan took his bag and sat behind the table. He looked at George and waited for the big announcement.

George stood, cleared his throat, and paused. "Ladies and gents, you are about to see the dazzling magic of Yan, the Master of the Dark Arts. He will amaze and astonish you!"

Yan smiled. "Watch carefully while I take an ordinary glass and an ordinary quarter." He held these up for the imaginary audience to see. "Next I wrap the glass in a piece of newspaper." Yan wrapped the glass in the piece of newspaper, twisting the paper at the bottom of the glass to hold it in place. "Now watch." He put the newspaper-covered glass over the coin. "Who'd like to guess whether the coin on the table is showing heads or tails?" He glanced around. "Ricky?"

Ricky called out and made a guess. "Tails," he said.

Yan lifted the glass and revealed the coin. "Come see. Were you right?"

"Yeah," Ricky said, walking up and looking down at the coin on the table.

Yan flipped the coin over several times in rapid succession and quickly covered it again with the glass. "Want to try to make it two in a row?"

"Sure," Ricky said. "I'll guess heads this time."

Yan again whipped away the glass and uncovered the coin. He looked at it. "Right again," he said. "Let's go for three in a row." Yan again put the glass over the coin. But this time he stopped and looked puzzled. "Oh-oh," he said, as he smashed his hand down on the table. The glass had disappeared. All that remained on top of the table was a piece of crumpled newspaper. Yan reached underneath the table and pulled out the missing glass. "Sometimes I forget how powerful I am. I knocked that glass clear through the table," Yan said with a grin. Quickly he took a bow.

"Hey! That's a good trick," George said. "How did you.... Oh, never mind. I know, a magician never gives away any secrets." Again, George stood and cleared his throat. "And now for your further entertainment and amazement, I present Ricky the Remarkable!"

Yan came back to sit on the couch as Ricky walked up to the

table. Ricky brought with him a fully inflated balloon in one hand and a needle in the other. "I need a volunteer," Ricky said.

Yan promptly stood. "Ah, there's a brave young man," Ricky said. "I just want you to come up here and prick yourself with this needle to assure everyone that it's really sharp. Now don't hurt yourself," Ricky said, handing Yan the needle. "I don't want you to bleed to death. Just test it for sharpness."

Yan obligingly pricked himself with the needle and gave a loud yelp. "It's sharp," he testified.

At that moment, Ricky thought he heard a sound up on the stairs leading down to the basement. Was it his mom? Annabelle? "Did you guys hear something?" Ricky hurried over to the foot of the stairs, certain that he heard more scurrying sounds. He got to the foot of the stairs just in time to see a small pink dress disappear as the door closed. Annabelle had been spying on them.

Ricky came back to the table and said, "Now watch closely, ladies and gentlemen." He took the needle from Yan, who sat back down. In a big motion, Ricky pushed the needle right into the balloon. He was careful to poke the needle into the piece of cellophane tape that he had carefully attached to the balloon earlier. Nothing happened.

"Oh, dear," Ricky said. "So sorry. I forgot to give the command. "Abracadabra, Balloon burst!" As he spoke, he pricked the balloon again, this time at a spot where there was no cellophane tape, and this time it popped with a loud bang.

George scratched his head. "I don't know how you did that. You guys are good. Boy, this is going to be so much fun! I can hardly wait for our trip to Camp Betasso." He grinned. "Why don't you say Abracadabra together, and maybe we can materialize right there!"

CHAPTER 14

When Ricky tromped upstairs to bed, he was still annoyed that Annabelle had sneaked down into the basement to spy on him and his friends practicing for the magic show. And he was pretty sure that she knew he had spotted her slipping away. She might have come down to plot to sabotage their acts Friday night. Ricky wasn't willing to give her the benefit of the doubt.

Before Ricky slipped into bed, he came up with an idea for payback. He laid out clean clothes for the morning on the chair, and he set his alarm clock. Ricky normally didn't set an alarm. He depended on his internal clock and woke up at the same time every day. However she did it, Annabelle always managed to wake up about ten minutes earlier than Ricky, and then she'd hog the bathroom all morning. Ricky decided this Wednesday would be different.

As soon as his alarm went off in the morning, Ricky silenced it, picked up his clothes, hurried into the bathroom, and locked the door. Then he took a long shower, toweled off, and was dressing in a leisurely fashion when he heard pounding on the door.

"Will you get out of there? Annabelle growled. "You're going to make me late."

Ricky didn't bother answering. He grinned as he carefully combed his hair. And he smiled even more broadly as he looked down at his sneakers, and stopped to slowly untie each shoe and re-tie the laces again, making sure the length of each lace after the bow was perfectly matched.

When he finally emerged from the bathroom, whistling a happy tune, Annabelle all but bowled him over as she rushed inside. Ricky went down to breakfast in a good mood. He had finished his usual two pieces of toast and jam before Annabelle came tearing down the stairs. She gave him a killer stare but didn't say anything.

Ricky continued whistling as he walked toward school. George ran out and joined him as he went by his house. This happened almost every day now, and Ricky was glad to have someone to walk to school with.

"I can hardly wait for Friday," George said. "We're going to have a blast all night in Owl Cabin up at Betasso. And you and Yan are going to wow them at the magic show."

The day at school went well. Only a few kids came running up today demanding to hear an account of the cougar attack. For the most part, that was old news, but things were different from the first day of school. Lots of kids waved at him now, or called "Hi, Ricky," as they passed. He was definitely no longer a stranger in the school.

In the early afternoon, big fluffy clouds began piling up, higher and higher in the sky, until they were impressive thunderheads. After lunch, the sun faded and the sky darkened. Then came the sound that Ricky dreaded to hear: a roll of thunder. He glanced at the clock above his teacher's desk, and he thought about Bones home alone out in the backyard. About quarter to three, the thunder became more frequent and lightning flashed across the sky.

A few minutes later, rain began, and then hail pelted down. It made a racket on the school roof, and kids stared through the windows of Mrs. Hannigan's classroom. Ricky thought about Bones and wondered if he'd taken shelter under a tree. The hail only lasted about five minutes. When the bell finally rang, most of the students hovered just inside the door in the hallways near the parking lot, hoping that parents would drive up to the school to rescue them. There was already a traffic jam leading to the school parking lot, and it was getting worse by the minute.

Not only was the area crowded with over three hundred kids coming out of the building and dozens of cars driving in, but the rain was coming down so hard that it was difficult to see.

"We'll wait here, under the overhang," George said to Ricky, just outside the school door. "I'm sure Mom is on her way to pick us up."

Ricky realized that it could be ten or fifteen minutes before Mrs. Schumacher could make it through the traffic jam. *Hold on, Bones*, he thought. *I'm coming.* He knew that getting a car back out on the road and home would be slow, too. Ricky couldn't afford to wait. By now his dog would be frantic, running around the yard.

Like all the other kids who'd set out for school on this warm August day, Ricky didn't have even a jacket, and it was still pouring. "I'm going to head home," he announced.

"You'll drown out there," George protested. "At least wait a few minutes until the rain lets up."

"Can't wait," Ricky said, and he rushed from under cover. It was a shock to feel the cold rain hit him full force in the face. Immediately he broke into a lope and went down the steps from the front lawn of the school. The intersection was blocked, and the traffic light was useless at this point. Ricky didn't wait for a green light. He threaded in and out of the cars, which were coming in three directions. Once across the street and onto the sidewalk, Ricky began to run full speed. He could hear the sloshing of his soaking wet sneakers as he sped home. The front of his red t-shirt got soaked through during the first two minutes, and his backpack and jeans weren't much better.

Two blocks from the school, Ricky caught sight of George's mother in her car, inching her way forward to the school. She motioned him to come get in, but he ran right on by. The moment he reached home, Ricky dropped his soaking backpack just outside the door and ran straight into the family room. He slid open the door to the back patio, calling, "Bones! Bones! Where are you?"

Peering through the rain, Ricky scanned the yard. Bones was nowhere to be seen. He hurried back inside and ran to the kitchen. There, in front of the pet door, he saw Bones's collar. With a sinking heart, Ricky realized that Bones must have tried hard to squeeze inside and had pulled off his collar as he was forced to retreat back out. Mike still had done nothing about enlarging the cat door.

Frantic, Ricky rushed into the backyard again. He was soaked through, and his hair was plastered to his face, but he no longer felt the outside cold. The cold was inside him now as fear gripped him. This time he checked behind every bush and tree. Could Bones be hiding somewhere, holed up seeking shelter? Even as he continued to search, Ricky knew Bones was not in the yard. He was out there somewhere, cold, scared, and alone.

CHAPTER 15

Ricky tore across the gravel path toward the backyard gate that ran along the side of the garage to the front of the house.

"Bones! Where are you, Bones?"

He stopped in dismay just short of the gate and stared down at the gravel. A hole burrowed through the gravel and dirt, right under the gate. It was now a mud puddle. Bones had dug his way out.

Ricky threw open the gate and rushed out to the front sidewalk. The rain had let up a lot by now. He looked up and down the street but could see no sign of a dog in either direction. Ricky ran down the hill, calling Bones's name. From the bottom of the block, he ran back up the street on the opposite side.

"Bones! Bones!" he kept shouting as he looked on each porch.

When he got back to the front of his own house, Ricky kept going up the hill. He met George and Mrs. Schumacher, who were pulling into their driveway.

"What's going on?" Mrs. Schumacher asked as she rolled down the window and looked at Ricky who was soaking wet.

"It's my dog, Bones. He's missing. He's terrified of thunder and lightning. He couldn't get in the house, so he dug his way out from under the gate, and he's run away."

"I'll help you hunt for him," George said, starting to climb out of the car.

"Wait!" Mrs. Schumacher called. "Get in the car, Ricky. Take off that wet shirt and wrap yourself in the blanket that's back there. I can drive while you two watch out the windows. We can cover more ground faster."

Ricky leapt into the back seat. He pulled off his wet shirt and wrapped the blanket around him. Slowly they drove up one street and down the next. George looked on one side while Ricky looked on the other. After their own street, they tried the streets on either side of them. They wove through street after street. There was no sign of Bones anywhere.

Finally Mrs. Schumacher said, "I think we'd better go home. Your mom and dad will be getting home soon, Ricky, and they're going to worry if you're not there."

By the time Mrs. Schumacher dropped Ricky off in his driveway, the rain had stopped, and the sun was trying to peek out again. She said, "Be sure to let me know if there's anything more I can do to help. Bones will probably come home now that the rain's stopped."

"Thanks," Ricky said. He didn't really believe her, but he clung to a bit of hope. He picked up his wet t-shirt and left the blanket he'd been wearing on the floor of the back seat.

Ricky hurried into his house. Annabelle had caught a ride home with one of her friends, and she was sitting dry and comfy in the family room, reading. Ricky took little notice of her, and she didn't look up as he hurried, shirtless, out into the backyard again. Could Bones have come home?

Ricky was still out in the yard searching when his mother drove into the garage.

"Ricky!" she called, sliding open the door when she caught sight of him. "Where's your shirt? You're soaked." Then looking around, she asked, "Where's Bones?"

Ricky ran over, and wet as he was, he grabbed his mother for a minute and buried his face, wet with rain and tears, into her shoulder. He was so scared. "He's run away. Bones is missing."

With his mom's arm around him, they walked back inside. Ricky told her how he'd searched for Bones first on foot and then in Mrs. Schumacher's car.

Annabelle heard all this, of course, but she pretended to be still reading, and she said nothing.

Mike got home and was quickly filled in on what had happened. "We'll call the Animal Shelter," Mike said. "Someone will call them, or check his dog tags and call us. I'm sure we'll be hearing something soon."

"No one's going to call us," Ricky said. He walked over to the kitchen table and picked up Bones's collar with his dog tags attached. "Bones tried to get inside through that cat door. Of course, it still isn't big enough for him, and he pulled off his collar when he backed out again. He's out there, wet and scared and without his dog tags."

Mike looked stricken. He slapped his forehead. "This is my fault," he said. "I knew I should put a bigger pet door there, and I kept putting it off while I did other things."

"Ricky," his mother said, "go upstairs, get dry, and put on some fresh clothes. I'll drive with you down the street to the park and wherever else we can think of. Surely Bones hasn't gone far. And,

Mike, you call the Animal Shelter and give them a description of Bones. Tell them that he's pulled off his collar and tags."

She turned to Annabelle who had finally put down her book. "Annabelle, you can call up all your friends who live near here. Tell them what happened and give them a description of Bones. Ask them to phone us if they see him."

Annabelle reluctantly stood and got her cell phone. She began calling.

Ricky changed as fast as he could. Then he joined his mother, and they set out in the car. Down at the park, they climbed out, split up, and each made a loop around the small lake. No sign of Bones.

Slowly they drove up and down all the neighboring streets again. Nothing. Discouraged, they finally drove back home.

"Maybe Mike or Annabelle has heard something," Ricky's mother said hopefully, and they climbed out of the car even though she knew if they had, they would have called her cell phone.

No one had heard anything.

"Someone will find him," Mike said. He put his hand on Ricky's shoulder, and Ricky shrugged it off. As Ricky did so, he caught the look of dismay on his mother's face.

"Could we call the vet now?" Annabelle asked.

Ricky turned to look at her. "The vet? Why would Bones go running to the vet's?"

"Not about Bones," Annabelle said. "About Darwin. I know your dog is missing. I've already pestered all my friends to keep an eye out for him while you were out searching. He'll be home soon, fine except for being wet. But remember my cat? The one that's half dead because he was attacked by a mountain lion?" She turned to her dad. "You said that we could check with the vet about Darwin this afternoon. You said you'd take me down to see him."

"Yeah, you can go ahead and call the vet, Belle. If he says it's okay, I'll drive you down for a quick visit before dinner. There's time, isn't there?" he asked turning to Ricky's mother. "And really there's nothing more we can do for Bones right now except wait for someone to find him."

Annabelle quickly called the vet's.

Ricky turned to his mother. "I've thought of one other place that Bones might have gone," he said. "Mole Hill. He just might have run up there since that's where we hike all the time. I'm going to walk up and take a look."

His mother said, "Okay, Ricky, but don't be gone long. I want everyone back here before six o'clock. I'll man the telephone while I get dinner on, and I hope I'll have good news by the time you get back."

Ricky hurried to get his hiking boots, and he picked up a jacket, too, just in case it started to rain again. He was out the door before Mike and Annabelle got in the car to go and visit Darwin. As he rushed toward the Open Space land, Ricky couldn't help but think of mountain lions. What if Bones ran into one that had wandered close to town?

As quickly as he could, Ricky walked to the trailhead and began to hike up on the open space land. His brow was furrowed, and he clenched his jaw. He was mad at Annabelle for never having thanked Bones for saving Darwin, and he was mad at Mike for never getting around to putting in a bigger pet door. He was mad at both of them for being so unconcerned about Bones. Even worse, deep, deep inside, he was mad at his mother for ever marrying Mike and moving them to Boulder.

Worse than the anger, though, was the fear. Fear that Bones was gone forever.

"Bones! Bones!" Ricky called his dog's name over and over as he climbed Mole Hill. With each passing minute, Ricky felt less and less hopeful that Bones had run this way. Still, he paused often to look in the mud for dog tracks. There were none.

Having gone up and down Mole Hill, Ricky turned for home. He kept thinking about his dog. He couldn't imagine life without Bones.

CHAPTER 16

Ricky trudged from the Open Space land, past the school, and home again. Desperately, he kept looking for Bones in each yard and on each porch as he walked by. When he got in front of George's house, the door flew open and George came running out.

"Any news?"

"No. No sight of him, and no one's called."

"He'll turn up," George said.

What if he doesn't? Ricky thought. But he didn't reply. He knew his friend was trying to keep up his spirits.

As Ricky crossed the street, he saw that Mike's car was already in the garage. Mike and Annabelle must be back from the vet's already. Ricky pulled off his muddy boots before entering the house. With only the faintest flicker of hope, Ricky glanced at his mom as he entered. Had anyone called? One look at her face told him. He didn't need to ask. Annabelle, all smiles, was mid-story recounting her latest visit to the vet, which she concluded by saying, "And Darwin is so-ooo much better. He'll be coming home soon."

Ricky wondered—would Bones ever be coming home again?

Ricky washed up, sat down at the table, and picked at his food. Every time he took a bite, he thought of Bones, out there somewhere, hungry and wet. Ricky's throat seemed to close up. Where could Bones be? Suddenly, through Ricky's cloudy brain, an idea shone through.

Mike was in the middle of describing a traffic jam he'd been caught in, but Ricky, who was paying little attention anyway, broke right in.

"Mom, do you think Bones might have headed back to our old house in Broomfield?"

Mike stopped talking and turned to look at Ricky. "That's more than twenty miles away," he said.

"And dogs only do things like that in TV shows and movies, not in real life," Annabelle said, rolling her eyes.

"It's a long shot," Ricky agreed. "But it does happen. Do you think he might have, Mom?"

"I know that the Andrews family moved into the house this week. I'll call information and get their new phone number tomorrow, let them know what happened, and ask them to be on the lookout for Bones."

"Tomorrow?" Ricky said. "Can't you call them right now?"

"I could, Ricky," his mother said, "but they're probably just sitting down to dinner. Even if Bones did decide to walk back to Broomfield and somehow found his way, he wouldn't be there yet."

"But he could get there tonight, or early in the morning. Couldn't you call them tonight? Please?"

"All right." His mother reached over to squeeze his arm. "I'll call right after dinner."

True to her word, as soon as the dishwasher was loaded, Ricky's mom called them. Ricky hovered nearby during the whole conversation.

When his mother hung up, she said, "Nice people. They're worried about Bones, and they've got our phone number, and they have a good description. They promised to call if they catch sight of him, and I said we'd call back when we found Bones."

Usually Ricky pushed bedtime boundaries a little, trying to stay up as late as he could, but not tonight. The mystery he had been eagerly reading yesterday wasn't interesting any more. The program he tried watching on television made no sense. Ricky headed up to bed without urging.

When Ricky opened his eyes in the morning, still half-asleep, something felt wrong. He was puzzled for a moment. He heard the usual sounds of Annabelle involved in her morning beauty routine in the bathroom, and the noises of his mother moving around in the kitchen below. Then it hit him. He sat upright. Bones! There was no Bones waiting to greet him at the foot of the bed. Guilt washed over Ricky. How could he forget about Bones, even when he was asleep?

Mechanically, Ricky pulled on some clothes, and after finally hearing Annabelle walk downstairs, he made a hasty trip to the bathroom, washed his face and ran a comb through his hair, and went down to the kitchen. He sat at the table and drank the milk and juice that his mother had set out for him.

"Honey, you've got to eat something," his mother said. "At least a piece of toast."

Ricky got up, popped a piece of toast, and buttered it. He took a bite, but he could barely swallow.

"We're certain to get some news of Bones today," his mother said.

"I'll phone the animal shelter during the noon hour to see if there's any news," Mike said.

"And I'm going to make a poster," Ricky's mother said. "I want to include a picture of Bones. Can you get me one?" she asked Ricky.

Glad to do something, anything to help, Ricky ran upstairs again and sat at his computer. He looked through several pictures. Looking through them caused a lump to rise in Ricky's throat. He finally picked one of Bones sitting on the grass of their old home in Broomfield. Ricky could see that Bones was happy. He printed it and ran back downstairs and handed it to his mother.

"Good," she said. "I'll get the poster made during lunch hour and take it to a copy shop. I'll pick them up right after school and come home early today. Come straight home after school, Ricky. We'll go out together and put the posters on telephone poles in the neighborhood, and anywhere else we can think of."

Just hearing about the plan helped. The thought of doing anything, however small, was better than doing nothing.

"And honey, Mike and I will be phoning each other back and forth today. If we learn anything about Bones, we'll call the school and have the school secretary take a note to you. I promise."

"Thanks, Mom."

Ricky left for school at his regular time, and George came running out to join him.

"Any news?" George asked.

"No."

George looked back at his mother who still stood in the doorway, apparently waiting for word about Bones. He shook his head at her, and she went back inside.

As they walked to school, George talked about Camp Betasso, clearly still excited about the prospect of a weekend of Outdoor Education, but Ricky had nothing to say. His enthusiasm for Outdoor Education had vanished along with Bones.

At school, hanging out around the back door before the bell rang, Ricky shared with his friends that his dog had gone missing.

"Bummer," Wally said.

"There's no more rain and thunder. It's real nice today. He's sure to come running home," Yan said. "And if this great weather continues, we're going to have two really nice days up at camp."

"I may not even be going to camp," Ricky said.

"Not going? What do you mean?" George asked. "Everybody goes on the Outdoor Ed trip."

"If Bones doesn't turn up today, I'm sure not going off to some camp Friday and Saturday. I'm going to stay right here and hunt for him."

The other members of Owl Cabin looked at Ricky in dismay.

"I'm sorry," Ricky said. "But if Bones isn't back, I'm not going."

CHAPTER 17

Fortunately for Ricky, there were no tests or big projects to-day. All he could think about was Bones. Every time some-one opened the door to the classroom, Ricky looked up. Could it be someone who was carrying a message to him from the office? It never was.

At lunch, Ricky picked at his spaghetti. He gave his chocolate chip cookie to George, his celery to Yan, and his carrot sticks to Wally.

While they were out on the playground, playing catch, Ricky heard a car screech to a sudden stop in front of the school. That opened up another stream of ugly thoughts. What if Bones had been running home after the storm and had been hit by a car? Would a driver stop? Would someone take him to a vet or to the animal shelter?

The ball that Wally threw whizzed right on by as Ricky stared out at the street.

Even though it was only Thursday, Mrs. Hannigan held a class meeting at the end of the day. "Be sure to check your list tonight so that you have everything you need," she reminded them. "And don't forget. Those of you who have signed up to perform magic, bring your supplies. Please be sure not to be late to school tomorrow. An hour after school starts, the buses will be here waiting for us. Any questions?"

Ricky had a question all right, but not for Mrs. Hannigan. Where was Bones? He kept his eye on the classroom clock, watching the long hand jerk forward a minute at a time. He could hardly wait to get home and scatter posters of Bones all over town. Someone must have seen him. This wasn't some magic show. Bones couldn't have disappeared into thin air.

The moment the school bell rang, Ricky was out the door. George rushed after him. He had agreed to jog home with Ricky and help put up lost dog posters. The two boys made it home in record time and didn't have long to wait for Ricky's mom to drive into the garage. She must have walked out the door of her classroom along with her students.

Ricky's mom hurried inside and opened up a small cardboard box to show George and Ricky the one hundred posters she'd picked up from the copy shop. They were bright colors of shocking pink, lemon yellow, and lime green. Each showed Bones sitting on the lawn, head cocked to one side, staring at the camera. Each offered a reward.

"These are great, Mom," Ricky said. "They're so bright, you can't help but notice them. Can we start putting them up right now?"

"Sure," she said. She scurried about getting a roll of tape, a small scissors, and a stapler. "You can go up and down our street. Fasten them onto telephone poles. Then come back. By then, I'll have our casserole in the oven, and I'll drive us around the park, and anywhere else we can think of."

"Okay." Ricky felt energized for the first time that day. He put the roll of tape around his wrist like a watchband and took a handful of posters. George carried the scissors and stapler. Up and down the block they went until every available pole sported a picture of Bones.

A few poles held tattered remnants of earlier signs for garage sales and one rain-streaked poster kept turning up for a lost cat. Ricky's heart tightened when he saw these. Was that cat ever found? Would Bones' picture be hanging here days or weeks from now with Bones still missing?

Ricky and George worked like a smooth team. George held a brightly colored poster around the pole while Ricky stapled and taped it in place.

When they got home, Ricky's mom was ready to go. She wrote a hurried note for Mike and Annabelle, leaving it on the kitchen table. Within minutes the three of them were out in the car, driving up and down neighboring blocks. After blanketing the neighborhood, they went to major intersections, and then drove over to post others on the bulletin boards in both the grocery store and the branch library.

They got back home just before Mike and Annabelle came driving back from their afternoon visit to the vet's.

George left for home, Ricky set the table, and his mother finished the rest of the dinner preparation.

Mike admired the left-over stack of posters that were near the kitchen sink. "Those posters are bound to help."

Annabelle barely glanced at the posters as she launched right into a description of how lively Darwin was today, and how quickly he was healing. "I got to ask more questions about being a veterinarian, too," she added. "That career report is going to be so easy."

Over dinner, as everyone chimed in to the conversation, Ricky bided his time. He knew he couldn't wait much longer to tell his mother that he wasn't going on the Outdoor Education trip tomorrow.

Annabelle had been packing her duffle bag since last Monday. She was constantly putting things in and taking things out. No one would ever guess she was packing for a day in the hills. It looked like she was going to Europe for a month.

Ricky hadn't packed a thing. Tuesday night he'd been practicing for the magic show, and since Bones disappeared, he'd completely lost all interest in Camp Betasso. But he knew that his mom would expect him to be packing everything tonight.

There was finally a lull in the conversation, and Ricky was about to break the news, when the phone rang. For a moment, Ricky froze. He looked at his mom. Was this the call they'd been waiting for?

Ricky's mother rushed to the phone. "Manders' residence."

She listened a moment, and then a great smile lit up her face. Ricky, who had been afraid to even hope that the call would be about Bones, felt his heart double its beat. He watched as his mother grabbed a pencil and jotted down an address.

"We'll be right over," she assured whoever was on the other end of the line. "And thank you, thank you, for calling us."

Hanging up, she rushed back to the table. "It was a Mr. Woodley who lives over on Darley Avenue," she said. "He saw our poster when he stopped at the grocery store this afternoon. And he just walked outside and found a beagle without a collar sniffing around in his next-door neighbor's yard. He says the dog is friendly and it looks just like Bones! He's keeping him there until we arrive."

"Let's go." Ricky pushed back his chair.

All four of them hurried out to Mike's car and drove to Darley

Avenue, about ten blocks away.

Ricky's eyes sparkled, but he was too excited to say a word.

"What's the reward?" Annabelle asked. "Your poster offered a reward."

"The reward is twenty-five dollars," Ricky's mom said, "but Mr. Woodley said he didn't want any reward. He just wanted to be sure this dog got home safely."

"Sounds like a good guy," Mike said. "I knew someone would be calling."

Once they got to Darley, they checked house numbers until they found the one they were looking for. Everyone tumbled out of the car and headed for the front door.

Mr. Woodley answered it. "Hello. You must be the Manders. I shut the dog in the garage. Thought that might be the best place for him till you got here. I took him some water and a leftover piece of meatloaf I had in the fridge. He gulped it down. That little guy's hungry."

Poor Bones, Ricky thought. That meat loaf might have been his first meal since Tuesday night.

Mr. Woodley shut the front door and led them to the garage where they all crowded around in front and watched as he entered the code to his automatic door opener. Slowly the door of the garage rolled up, rumbling as it went, and Ricky caught his first glimpse of the dog.

"Come here, Bones," Ricky called, kneeling down and reaching out.

The dog ignored him and ran over to Mr. Woodley, tail wagging, obviously hopeful for another piece of meat loaf.

Ricky stared in disbelief. It wasn't Bones.

CHAPTER 18

For a moment, Ricky couldn't speak. He stared at the beagle that was wagging his tail in front of Mr. Woodley. Stricken, Ricky looked up at his mom. From the look on her face, he knew she'd realized as quickly as he had that this dog was not Bones.

"I'm sorry, Mr. Woodley," Ricky's mom said. "Thank you, but it's not our dog. I so appreciate your being on the lookout and calling us, but this isn't Bones."

The happy smile disappeared from the man's face. "Oh, dear," he said. "I'm so sorry to have gotten your hopes up like that. I thought for sure he was yours." As he spoke, he knelt down and patted the dog. "He's such a friendly little guy. I'll call the animal shelter right away. Someone else must be looking for him."

As the man led the dog back into the garage, he said, "I'll keep my eyes open though, and good luck in finding your dog. Would you call me when you find him? I'd like to know."

Ricky wanted to thank him, but he couldn't speak. His mom put her arm around his shoulders, and they all started back to the car. Ricky fought to hold back tears.

"What a rotten break," Mike said as he climbed into the driver's seat. "And I was so sure someone had found Bones."

After Ricky buckled up in the backseat, he balled his hands into fists. Disappointment had turned to anger. If Annabelle made one wisecrack, he knew he'd smack her. But for once, Annabelle was silent.

When they got home, there was nothing Ricky wanted more than to rush upstairs to his room. He wanted to fling himself on his bed, beat on it, and cry at the same time. But he knew he had something else to do first.

"Mom," he said, as soon as they all walked into the kitchen to the messy table they'd left when they rushed out. "I'm not going on that Outdoor Education trip tomorrow."

"Everyone goes on the Outdoor Ed trip," Annabelle said. "Everyone."

"Not me," Ricky said. "I'm not going away with Bones still missing. I have to stay here and hunt for him."

"Let's sit down and talk about this," Mom said. Putting an arm around his shoulder, she led Ricky over to the couch and sat close to him. "Honey, I think I know how you feel. Bones is such an important part of our family. You're worried sick about him, and so are the rest of us."

Ricky doubted that. Oh, he knew his mom was worried, but he really doubted if Mike and Annabelle had even noticed that the dog they'd just gone to see wasn't Bones. Of course, Mike at least pretended to care. Annabelle didn't even bother to pretend.

"But right now," his mom went on, "there's not a lot more that we can do. We've called the new people who moved into our old house, notified the animal shelter, phoned the neighbors, put up posters, and we'll follow up every lead. I can't think of anything else to do. Now comes the really hard part—waiting. But staying home and missing an important part of school won't help."

"Why should I bother to go?" Ricky said. "All I'd do there is worry about Bones."

"Actually, it'll make the waiting time go faster. You'll be taking part in a lot of activities. They'll help you take your mind off of Bones."

"Nothing could take my mind off of Bones," Ricky said. How could his mother of all people think that?

Mike spoke up. "Look. I'm sure Bones is going to be home real soon. Your mom's right. There's no need for you to change school plans. We'll phone you up there and let you know the minute he gets home."

"Oh, sorry, Dad. But you can't phone us," Annabelle said. "We can't take phones or any electronic devices with us. It says so in capital letters on our information sheet."

"This will be an exception," Ricky's mom promised. "I'll call Mrs. Hannigan right now and explain what's going on."

Ricky sighed. He knew he had lost the battle. Briefly, he thought about running away himself; not for long, just until after the bus left tomorrow morning. He could sneak out tonight after everyone had gone to bed. But Ricky knew that would just about kill his mother. And he knew first-hand how terrible it was to have someone you love missing. He couldn't do that.

He'd have to go. He was stuck. But he sure wasn't going to be a happy camper.

At least he didn't have kitchen duty tonight. He left Annabelle with the mess on the table to clear up and went upstairs to pack. He dug out the information sheet and began making a stack on the bed of everything he needed. He was pretty far along with his packing when his mother came up to his room.

"I've talked with Mrs. Hannigan, and she was really sorry to hear about Bones. She gave me her cell phone number and said that I can call her at any time, and she'll report any news to you. Even if we get another lead that doesn't pan out, I'll call and give you a report. I promise you won't miss a thing."

Ricky didn't bother to look up. He grimly continued with his packing.

"And furthermore," his mom went on, and she managed a smile at this point, "she gave me permission to drive up to Camp Betasso when we find Bones, and let him visit with you for a few minutes."

Ricky noticed that his mom had said, "*when* we find Bones," not "*if* we find Bones." He took heart at that.

"So whenever we find him, you'll see him almost as fast as we do. We'll put him in the car and drive right to the camp. I think that was pretty nice of Mrs. Hannigan," she went on. "So I hope while you're up there, you'll show you appreciate it by participating. We're counting on that."

"Okay," Ricky said, without looking up.

His mother glanced at the bed. "Looks as if you've made a great start on your packing. Do you need any help?"

"No, thanks," After she left, he stood there for a minute. Tears welled up again. Brushing his hand across his eyes, he methodically packed up, even remembering everything he needed for the magic show. He wished he were a real magician who could make Bones suddenly appear.

Ricky finished packing and went downstairs where he half-watched a dumb TV show. He could hear Annabelle on her cell phone, yakking to one of her friends about pink butterfly paja-mas.

When the house phone rang, Ricky held his breath. Could it be? Was someone calling about Bones?

Mike answered and said, "It's for you, Ricky. It's George."

Deflated again, Ricky walked over, took the phone. "Hi."

"Hi," George responded. "My mom is driving you and me and Annabelle to school tomorrow with all our camp gear. I wanted to remind you to bring the magic stuff." There was an awkward pause before he went on. "I'm glad you're coming, Ricky. Even though you're so worried about Bones. I know he's going to come home, soon, I know it!"

I wish I knew that, Ricky thought, but all he said was, "Okay. See you in the morning."

CHAPTER 19

Even though he hadn't wanted to go to school at all this morning, Ricky felt a little surge of excitement as all his classmates picked up their overnight gear and walked from the classroom out to the parking lot. Mr. Bennett's class was already assembling halfway across the lot, crowding around their own bus. Wally had managed to squeeze and push his way to the very front of the line for Mrs. Hannigan's class. Ricky knew Wally's plan was to muscle his way into the bus first and claim the very back seat for them.

Mrs. Hannigan walked to the front of the line, knocked on the closed bus door to alert the driver they were ready to load, and said, "Class, this is our driver for today, Mr. Conley."

A smiling, bald bus driver opened the doors and stood hanging out at the top of the steps to give a wave and call "Hi" to the group.

Mrs. Hannigan continued, "He's going to store all the duffle bags in the back of the bus first. So, one by one, I want you to come up and hand me your bag. I'll pass it to Mr. Conley, and he'll stow it safely on the floor and seats in the back." *Poof* went their plan of sitting in the very back seat.

Like an assembly line, the duffle bags were brought forward and stowed. Clearly Mrs. Hannigan had done this before. It took only a few minutes. Then there was a big surge as everyone climbed aboard. Wally and Yan sat right behind George and Ricky. Ricky sat by the window, and once the bus pulled out of the parking lot and headed for the highway, he kept looking out, hoping to catch sight of Bones. It was silly to hope, but Ricky couldn't help it.

"Hah!" said Wally with satisfaction, as he leaned forward and glanced out the window. "We didn't get the back seat, but at least we're ahead of Bennett's class. We'll get to Camp Betasso first."

Who cares? Ricky thought, but he didn't say anything to dampen Wally's enthusiasm.

The trip was less than an hour, but it seemed to Ricky that it was taking twenty-five years to get there. When they went through Broomfield, their route took them within a few blocks of Ricky's old house. He felt a twinge of homesickness, and kept staring out the window, hoping to see Bones trotting down the familiar blocks. Finally they left the main highway and bounced down a gravel road to the camp site. After they parked in the lot in front of the main lodge, Mrs. Hannigan called out cabin assignments and gave instructions.

"Wait outside the bus while Mr. Conley and I unload your gear. Then pick up your things and stow them in your cabins." She glanced at her watch. "By ten thirty sharp, meet me back here, just inside the main lodge, and I'll give you all today's schedule."

Although it was only mid-morning, it was already hot when they climbed out of the bus, waited for their duffle bags, and finally set out to find Cabin Six. Ricky noticed there were clusters of half a dozen cabins, with a boys' and girls' washroom located in the middle of each cluster. Making a stop, they checked out the toilets, showers, and wash basins.

Threading his way among the ponderosa pines, Yan suddenly called, "Here's Owl Cabin, Cool! It's out here on the very edge with almost no neighbors."

The four boys entered their small cabin. Ricky was immediately struck by the smell of redwood coming from the cabin in the warm August sun. He looked around at the four bunks, a small table with four chairs, and a chest of drawers. The one big window was covered by a thick green drape dotted with pictures of brown pine cones.

"I get a top bunk," Wally yelled.

"Me, too," said Yan.

Whatever, thought Ricky as he plopped down on one of the bottom bunks.

During the next several minutes, the boys settled in. They rolled out their sleeping bags on their bunks, and each claimed a drawer in the chest to stow away some of their stuff. Ricky took the bottom drawer. There was an old sheet stored in there, but he didn't need much room anyway. They left the rest in the duffle bags and stashed them over in one corner.

"Home Sweet Home," George said, looking around in satisfaction. He pulled open the short drape and looked out into the woods.

Ricky couldn't care less. He lay back on his bunk and thought about Bones.

"We'd better head over to the main lodge," George said. "It's almost time to meet Mrs. Hannigan."

As they walked back among the cabins to the lodge, Ricky saw

Annabelle and her buddies leaving Cabin Twelve. Idly he wondered if she and her ditsy friends had already pinned pink felt butterflies to their drapes. On entering the lodge, Ricky caught Mrs. Hannigan's eye. She smiled and gave a short shake of her head. No messages yet.

Everyone got a schedule. The planned activities mingled kids from both classes. There were two before lunch, one after lunch, and free time before dinner. On Saturday morning, there was another activity and then a hike. Everyone also had assigned duties—setting and clearing the tables, doing dishes, or helping prepare lunch, dinner, or breakfast.

Ricky's first activity was orienteering led by Mr. Bennett. The group was divided into four smaller groups. Each group had a map and a compass. The object was to visit each control point, in order, and to complete the course in the shortest amount of time. Each group was timed.

Next Ricky collected and examined rocks in a group led by a geology volunteer from the university. They identified different kinds of rocks and performed a hardness test on them. Both sessions were interesting, but every time Ricky found himself starting to get involved, an image of Bones flashed in his head, and he lost focus.

After geology, Ricky hooked up with George and Yan again. They compared notes as they headed over to eat at the main lodge. Wally had gone ahead, because he'd been given the job of helping prepare lunch. The meal was pretty simple, served cafeteria style.

After lunch, Ricky went with a group led by Mrs. Riggs for a sketching activity. First, she demonstrated some simple techniques. Then, with charcoal, paper, and a clipboard, they each chose a spot to sit and sketch. Some people did close ups of rocks, wildflowers and trees, while others chose vistas of the hills and distant mountains. Mrs. Riggs walked around offering encouragement.

Ricky felt pretty silly sitting all alone next to a rock, and he was glad when the hour ended. His drawing more or less looked like a rock. What more could you ask? Mrs. Riggs excused the group, reminding them that they had free time now until dinner.

"It's your only free time for the whole weekend," she reminded them. "So enjoy it. And remember, if you decide to do something outside your cabin or the main lodge, such as taking a hike, you must be with your buddy. No one wanders around alone."

Ricky walked back to Owl Cabin and found George was already there. Yan and Wally arrived shortly afterwards.

"So what'll we do with our free time?" Wally asked.

"How about going for a hike?" George suggested. "Taking along snacks, of course," he added walking over to his drawer to pull out a bag of chips. "I think everyone is headed for Arrowhead Hill. It seems to be the favorite spot."

"Good idea," Yan agreed, and he fished out a bag of unshelled peanuts. "I doubt there are any arrowheads left, after all the kids who've camped up here, but who knows? We might get lucky. Or maybe we can find some chipmunks, or something."

Wally went to his drawer and pulled out a bag of cookies. "Count me in."

Ricky was sitting on the bed, and he realized he hadn't even thought about bringing snacks. But that didn't matter. He wasn't hungry, and he didn't want to go hiking for two hours. What if Mrs. Hannigan got news about Bones and wanted to reach him?

"I think I'll stay here and take a snooze," Ricky said.

"Oh, c'mon," Yan coaxed. "It'll be fun."

"You guys go ahead." Ricky stretched out on his bunk.

The others left, and Ricky lay there for a while. He couldn't get to sleep, though. He kept imagining Bones hurt, Bones limping home, Bones penned up in a stranger's yard.

He was startled by a loud knocking on the cabin door. Who could that be? Maybe it was Mrs. Hannigan with news.

Ricky jumped up and ran to open the door. His hopes were dashed when he saw Kelly, Christa, and Beth standing there.

"What do you want?" Ricky asked. He wasn't in the mood for conversation with butterflies.

Christa spoke up. "Do you know where Annabelle is?"

"Annabelle?" Ricky said. "I thought she was sharing a cabin with you."

"She is," Christa said. "We've been doing our nails." She proudly wiggled her pink-tipped fingernails which until then she'd held out in front of her while they still dried.

"But Annabelle already did her nails last night, and she got mad and said we were wasting free time, and she stomped outside," Kelly said. "Now she's disappeared. She's my buddy, and she's not supposed to go off without me."

"That was fifteen minutes ago, and we can't find her anywhere," Beth said. "We thought she might have come down to bug you."

"Nope. Haven't seen her," Ricky said.

And you can bug off, he thought, as he closed the door and went back to his bunk.

About ten minutes later, there was another knock on his door. Ricky's heart raced and he hurried to open it. Again it was Christa, Kelly and Beth.

"We can't find her anywhere," Christa said. "We went and told Mrs. Hannigan, so she's going to get in trouble for going without a buddy. But Mr. Bennett hasn't seen her, and we're worried. Will you help us hunt for her?"

"Hunt where? This is a big place." Ricky thought for a moment and then added, "Did you check the bathroom? She can spend a lot of time in there."

"Of course we checked there," Beth said.

"And we searched the main lodge," Kelly added. "Now we're going to look in the woods. Maybe at Arrowhead Hill."

Ah, Ricky thought. *So that's why they're here. They're afraid to go into the woods by themselves.* He was feeling a little worried and guilty now, but he sure wasn't about to spend his free time walking around in the woods with three girls looking for Annabelle.

Ricky said, "Good luck."

He closed the door and lay back down. In spite of brushing them off, he did have a flicker of concern. Bones was missing, and now apparently Annabelle had disappeared, too. And that was strange. Even if she was mad at her friends, Annabelle wouldn't wander far into the woods alone.

Ricky went over to the main lodge. He found Mrs. Hannigan.

"Have you heard anything about Bones?" he asked.

"No, sorry. No word yet. By the way, have you seen Annabelle?

"No," Ricky said. "Her buddies are looking for her though."

Ricky walked back out of the lodge again. He felt uneasy and a little guilty about not helping find Annabelle. Suddenly Ricky remembered that night at the kitchen table last week when they'd been talking about going to Camp Betasso. Annabelle had said that her older friend, Melanie, told her that Lily Pond was "to die for," and was "the most beautiful place on earth." Would Annabelle have decided to hike down there? During the orienteering activity, Ricky had seen a map of the whole Camp Betasso area and he'd noticed Lily Pond. It wasn't far.

Ricky walked over to Cabin Twelve. He wanted to suggest that the girls look for Annabelle at Lily Pond. But no one was in Cabin Twelve. Apparently, the three butterflies had fluttered off to search on their own, at Arrowhead Hill or who knew where.

Ricky went back to his cabin. He felt guilty lying there. He at least had a clue as to where she might be. No one else did. He couldn't sleep anyway, so he might as well stretch his legs and walk down to Lily Pond. Of course, now he didn't have a buddy to go with him since George was off hiking with Yan and Wally. He wrote a note and left it on his cot saying where he'd gone. Then he took his water bottle, tied a sweatshirt around his waist, and set out.

Ricky walked behind the main lodge to a trailhead and took the trail across the meadow that led east. After about fifteen minutes, the trail split again, and Ricky took the one marked Lily Pond.

It was a lot darker now than it had been earlier, and Ricky studied the sky. Were they in for an afternoon thunderstorm? He hurried faster. In another twenty minutes, he reached the pond. He couldn't see anyone at all and felt a little silly for having come. He turned around and headed back to camp. Maybe if he hurried, he'd beat the thunderstorm.

Then he heard someone shout, "Help! Over here!"

CHAPTER 20

"**O**ver here!"

Ricky heard the shout again. He ran along the path that circled the pond. Suddenly he saw her. Annabelle was sitting on a log.

Ricky ran up and looked at her in disgust. All of her friends were worried and out searching for her, and here she sat, looking at the lily pads. But when he got close enough, he could see that Annabelle was crying.

"What's wrong?" he asked.

"My ankle," she said, rolling up her pant leg. Ricky could see that her ankle was swollen and blue. "It really hurts. I can't walk on it."

Ricky bent down for a closer look. "It sure doesn't look good." He reached out and touched it.

"Ouch!"

Ricky didn't prod any further. "I don't know if it's sprained or broken. What happened?"

"I came down here to look at Lily Pond. It's the one thing I wanted to see up here, and this was our only free time. Beth and Christa and Kelly wanted to do their nails. So I came alone. I was right over there." She pointed. "Just looking, when I heard something in the water right behind all those reeds at the edge of the pond. I saw ripples on the water, and it was coming closer and closer. I mean I thought it might be an alligator or something like the Loch Ness Monster. It was headed right for me, and I got scared."

An alligator—in Colorado, Ricky thought. *Could Annabelle be that dumb?* But aloud, he asked, "What did you do?"

"I ran over to that tree," Annabelle pointed to a nearby ponderosa pine, "I climbed up so it couldn't reach me. I waited a while, and when I thought it was safe, I jumped down. I landed wrong. My ankle felt really bad. I've tried to walk, but it hurts too much."

Ricky noticed then that Annabelle was shivering.

"Here," he said. He untied his sweatshirt and gave it to her. She quickly put it on.

"Did you ever see what it was that scared you?"

Annabelle looked down at the ground, and didn't answer.

"Come on. What was it?" Ricky insisted. "You must have seen it from up in the tree."

"Do you promise not to laugh?" Annabelle asked.

"I promise," Ricky said, wondering what tale she'd have to tell.

"It was a turtle," Annabelle confessed.

"A turtle?" Ricky's mouth twitched, but he managed not to laugh.

"Yeah, and not even a really big one. It crawled around for a minute and then swam back out again."

Ricky shook his head. Only Annabelle would be scared by a turtle. He thought of several wisecracks he might make, but Annabelle looked chilled, miserable, and in pain. So instead, he said, "You know, it's getting late, and I think it's going to rain. Your friends are worried because you're missing. We can't stay here. Let's see if you can walk holding onto me."

Annabelle stood and put her left hand up on Ricky's shoulder. He couldn't help but feel a little uncomfortable, but there was no other choice. He tentatively put his right hand around her waist. "Can you sort of hop along?"

'Yeah," Annabelle said. "I think so."

"Then let's go."

As they started back along the trail, the sky darkened.

Ricky stepped on a loose rock and stumbled a little. That quickly brought his thoughts back to Annabelle. From the look on her face, he knew that sudden lurch had hurt. Miraculously though, Annabelle clamped her mouth shut and wasn't complaining. He admired that, but he realized this was no time to let his mind wander. He had to keep his eyes on where he was stepping.

It was slow going, but they finally made it back up to the fork in the trail before the first drops fell, making deep polka-dots in the dust.

"Let's head for that clump of trees," Ricky said. "We can take shelter there."

Huddled close against the tree trunk of a huge fir tree, in the middle of a cluster of pines, they kept pretty dry. The arching branches of the fir made a roof of fine needles overheard.

Ricky helped Annabelle ease to the ground with her back

against the rough tree bark. He offered her a drink from his canteen. "You don't want to get dehydrated."

She took the canteen from him, but stared at the ground. Finally, she looked up and briefly smiled, then looked away again and took a small sip.

The rain pelted down.

"It's only fifteen minutes from here to the lodge," Ricky said. "I could go on ahead and get some people to come down here and carry you on a stretcher. It would be a lot easier on you."

"No," Annabelle said quickly. "The rain will let up in a few minutes, and I can make it. I'd die of embarrassment to be carried in on a stretcher."

Ricky knew he'd feel the same way, but he said, "Hey! When you're hurt, that's nothing to be embarrassed about."

For five minutes, the rain continued pelting down, but except for an occasional drip or two, Ricky and Annabelle remained dry under the fir tree. Then the rain let up and stopped.

"We can leave now," Ricky said.

Annabelle looked at Ricky pleadingly. "Before we go, you've got to promise not to tell anyone, ever, ever, that I climbed that tree to get away from a turtle."

Ricky remembered how Annabelle had carried on when he and Bones got skunked. He was looking forward to spreading the turtle story. He'd love describing how Annabelle clambered up the tree thinking she'd spied the Loch Ness Monster only to find out it was a little turtle. Ricky thought back to how good it felt to be the brave "lion kid," but he knew being called the scared "turtle kid" wouldn't be much fun.

"Remember how you and your friends carried on after poor old Bones and I got skunked? You held your noses while you walked by me in the school cafeteria. How do you think that felt?"

Annabelle had tears in her eyes. "I know. I was awful. And I've made fun of you for talking Spanish, and I've complained about your music and Maria's cooking. But you've got to promise," she insisted. "I know I've been a jerk. But it's been hard having you and Bones walk in and take over my house. Everything changed. I couldn't really complain to Dad or to Maria. So I guess I just took it out on you and Bones."

Ricky kept silent. Was Annabelle actually apologizing?

"And when that mountain lion came and almost killed Darwin, I was scared and so angry. I know I should have been thankful that Bones came to the rescue, but I couldn't stop blaming him. I'm sorry, Ricky." She paused. "And I really do hope Bones comes home, soon. When he does, I'll tell him I'm sorry, too."

Ricky released a big breath, blowing out a lot of anger and hurt. He found himself relaxing. Annabelle had been as miserable as he was. All he'd ever wanted was an apology to Bones.

"Okay," Ricky said, "I promise. So what *is* your story?"

"The truth," Annabelle said. She hesitated, "But not the whole truth. I'm leaving one part out. After all, the turtle didn't really *do* anything. So there's no need to mention it. I'll say I came down to Lily Pond, I climbed a tree, jumped down, hurt my ankle and couldn't walk back alone."

While they had talked, not only had the rain stopped, but in that miraculous way Colorado summer weather has, the sky had lightened, and the sun came out again.

"Okay," Ricky promised. "Your turtle story is safe with me. Someday when you're a well-known vet, you can share the story about how you were treed by a turtle in fifth grade."

Annabelle had to laugh at that thought. "And I really will try to behave better," she promised. "Maria is really a good cook. It'll just take me a while to get used to different foods." She smiled.

"But I don't think I'll ever share your taste in music."

"That's okay. I'm never going to share yours, either," Ricky said.

"I haven't liked sharing my dad," Annabelle admitted, "but at least I didn't have to leave my house and school and friends. Dad and Maria would be happy, I think, if maybe we tried a little harder to get along. Truce?" She stuck out her hand and Ricky shook it.

They grinned at each other. Ricky realized that she did understand how hard it had been, probably better than anyone else. And it felt good to share a secret.

Moving slowly, they made it up the hill to the main lodge. It was almost six. Everyone was gathering for dinner, and as soon as kids saw them, word spread quickly. Ricky and Annabelle were surrounded by people. Christa, Kelly and Beth all talked at once, offering tons of medical advice. Christa thought they should wrap the ankle in green leaves but she wasn't sure what kind. Kelly thought it needed a heating pad, and Beth said ice was needed.

Mrs. Hannigan and Mr. Bennett soon came and took over.

"Come on," Mr. Bennett said, lending Annabelle an arm. "We'll have the nurse take a look at that ankle."

As Annabelle limped off to see the nurse, accompanied by her three buddies, Ricky was left on the front porch of the lodge explaining about the ankle to latecomers. Knowing full well that the Loch Ness Monster story would be a lot more fun, Ricky stuck to Annabelle's version.

In a few minutes, Ricky went inside to find out how serious Annabelle's ankle injury was. The nurse said that although it was a bad sprain, nothing was broken.

Later, while Ricky was finishing dinner, Mrs. Hannigan came walking toward him. Catching sight of her, Ricky's heart raced. Was there finally news of Bones?

"No news about your dog, Ricky," Mrs. Hannigan said right away. "I called up your folks to tell them that Annabelle had sprained her ankle, and I asked if they wanted us to send her home or keep her here. Since Annabelle very much wanted to stay, they agreed. They asked me to tell you that they had placed an ad in the newspaper and that several friends were spreading the news through Facebook and blogs. They wanted to keep you up to date."

"Thanks, Mrs. Hannigan," Ricky said.

"They also want you to know that they are proud to hear how you helped Annabelle get through the rainstorm and back to camp." She paused and smiled. "I'm proud of you, too, even though you broke the rule about buddies."

Ricky's face reddened.

"But he left a note, Mrs. Hannigan," George said. "And it was sort of an emergency."

"Yes," Mrs. Hannigan agreed, "and if there's any news about your dog, Ricky, I'll let you know right away."

Ricky poked at his food with his fork. He thought, when Annabelle was missing and hurt, it had been so quick and easy to find her. Why was it taking so long for anyone to find Bones?

CHAPTER 21

After dinner, it was Ricky's turn to help clean up in the kitchen. As he scraped plates he wondered about Bones. Did Bones have dinner tonight? Had Bones been outdoors during another storm? Was he wet and cold and miserable? Ricky stood there for a moment. His heart ached with worry.

"Hey! Hurry up! Tonight's the night." Yan elbowed him back to the work at hand, and Ricky quickly finished scraping the plates.

The moment they were finished, Ricky and Yan hurried over to the cabin. They gathered the supplies they needed for their magic acts and rushed back to the main lodge.

The big meeting room had a raised stage platform at one end. On the stage was one chair and a table covered in a white cloth. No seats had been set up for the audience; the kids sat cross-legged on the floor. Annabelle was the exception. She sat like a queen on her throne, near a side wall, with a footstool on which she rested her ankle. Christa, Beth, and Kelly, her faithful ladies in waiting, huddled close to her. Ricky thought she might not be treated quite so royally if everyone knew she was "turtle girl."

Ricky sat with Wally, George and Yan. At one point he caught Annabelle's eye, and she actually smiled at him.

Mr. Bennett and Mrs. Hannigan were in a huddle. Then they scanned the seated audience. When Mrs. Hannigan caught Ricky's eye, she crooked her finger and beckoned him. *Was this it? News of Bones at last?* Ricky handed his blown-up balloon and his needle to Wally. In his haste to get up to Mrs. Hannigan, Ricky trod on a few fingers as he scrambled across bodies.

"Hi, Ricky." Seeing the eager look on his face, Mrs. Hannigan was quick to add, "No, there's no news about Bones."

Ricky's heart sank.

"Marko the Magnificent can't come," Mrs. Hannigan went on. "His wife has taken ill, and he's at the hospital with her. They're going to do an appendectomy, and he called to cancel. But he's promised to come to the school in a couple of weeks and do a show for us."

Oh, no! Ricky thought. This whole Magic Night was his idea. Now it was ruined.

Mr. Bennett handed the sign-up sheets from both classes to Ricky. "We really don't need Marko the Magnificent tonight," he said with a reassuring smile. "There are so many kids that signed up to do magic tricks that we'll be fine without him. But since Marko isn't here to call up the young magicians, and since you're a magician yourself, we wanted to ask you to be master of ceremonies and run the show tonight. What do you say? Will you save the day?" Mr. Bennett grinned at him.

"Me?" croaked Ricky.

"You'll be fine, Ricky," Mr. Bennett said. "And there are a dozen acts from each class. So how about it?"

Ricky hated to be up in front of people, but he felt he had no choice. He was the one who had suggested Marko the Magnificent, and he felt that Magic Night was his responsibility.

"Okay," Ricky said. His stomach lurched like an elevator and dropped to his feet.

"Great! Let's get started." Mrs. Hannigan led Ricky to the center of the stage and announced the change in plans. At first there was a low groan of disappointment. Ricky wished the stage would magically open up and swallow him. That didn't happen, so he took over.

"Hey! Don't be disappointed," he said. "We have twenty-four magicians waiting to perform for you tonight. Come on. Let's give them a hand and get started." He clapped and the audience quickly joined in.

Ricky, who had hoped he wouldn't have to say a word on stage, found himself announcing each act. He alternated going down the sign-up list, calling on someone from Mr. Bennett's class and then from Mrs. Hannigan's class. To his surprise, each act was pretty good. He had saved Yan for last, knowing his act was solid. Finally he called on him.

George walked up onto the stage with Yan. While Yan settled at the table, George began his introduction. "Ladeeeez and gentlemen. You are in for an awesome treat. I present to you Yan, the Great! Yan, the Mysterious. His magic will amaze and astonish you."

George scurried back to his place as Yan went into action. Yan talked about his ordinary glass and ordinary quarter, called on some kids to guess whether the quarter was head or tails and then made the "ordinary glass" seem to go right through the table. It all went smoothly, much as it had during rehearsal at Ricky's house. The audience applauded, and Yan took a bow and returned to his spot. As he sat down, Wally pounded on his back.

After the last act, Ricky gave a sigh of relief. "That's it," he said. Let's give all these magicians a big hand."

But before the audience could respond, Mrs. Hannigan leaped up and said, "Oh, no! Not yet. We have one more magician who signed up to perform tonight. Ricky, it's your turn!"

Trapped, Ricky stood there. Now Ricky was going to be the big finale—or the big fiasco. George came up on stage and handed the balloon and needle to Ricky.

Warmed up by now and not so scared to speak, George embellished his introduction. "I take pride in presenting to you Ricky, the Remarkable, the Sophisticated, the Sneaky, the Snappy, the Scintillating Master Magician!" George made a sweeping gesture over to Ricky.

Ricky bowed, his audience applauded, and he moved forward. "Tonight I will share with you my amazing needle. First, I need a volunteer."

Hands shot up, and Ricky called on a tall, skinny kid from Mr. Bennett's class who was wildly waving his arm.

"You sir, you in the bright blue t-shirt," Ricky said, "Please come up. I want you to carefully test this needle. Don't stab yourself. We don't want anyone bleeding in here. Just touch it gently and tell me if it's sharp."

"Ow!" the volunteer cried after pricking himself. "It's sharp."

"All right," Ricky said, dismissing his volunteer. "I will now stick this magic needle into my balloon. Ready?"

Several of the kids in front near the stage put their hands over their ears. Ricky took his needle, flourished it through the air, and in plain sight of everyone, he pricked the balloon. Nothing happened. A few murmurs rose from the crowd.

"So sorry," Ricky said. "I forgot to give my obedient needle the magic words. Needle, needle shining bright, pop this big balloon tonight. Abracadabra!"

Ricky waved his hand over the needle several times while staring at it. Finally, with a grand gesture, he pricked the balloon again. This time it gave a satisfying bang!

After bowing to loud applause, Ricky, took his seat on the floor. Glancing over at Annabelle, he saw her give him a thumbs up.

Mr. Bennett complimented all the magicians. He wished everyone a good night, reminding them that breakfast was eight o'clock sharp and telling them to get a good night's sleep because tomorrow was going to be a busy day.

Everyone surged toward the exit. As they passed near, several said "nice job" to Ricky, who felt proud and relieved that the show was over. He craned his head over the crowd, looking for Mrs. Hannigan. She caught his eye and shook her head. The little bit of joy that Ricky had felt momentarily from his success of Magic Night disappeared. Once again, he felt the cold ache of missing Bones.

Everyone came pouring out of the main lodge and scattered to the cabins. Most had brought flashlights. Few of the lights were ever focused on the paths. Everyone had fun shining the lights in everyone else's face. As the flashlights began spreading out among the cabins, Ricky thought they looked like the eyes of wild animals stalking through the trees. He thought of Bones again. Was Bones wandering lost on Mole Hill being stalked by the mountain lion? Where was Bones on this dark night?

Once they were back inside their cabin, Yan asked, "Now, what'll we do? This is Owl Cabin, and that means we definitely can't go to sleep before midnight."

Wally said, "I think we should wait a little bit for everything to settle down. Then we can sneak out to the girls' cabins and terrify them."

"I brought my Monopoly set," George said. "Maybe we could play while we're letting things settle down."

"Okay," Yan agreed quickly; so they soon settled into a game.

Every few minutes, Wally popped up and took a look outside to see what was going on. He reported on how many cabins still had lights on.

When for about the tenth time, Wally ducked in and out, he said, "Most of the cabins are dark now. Let's get down to something fun."

"Who's our target?" Yan asked. "The Butterflies?"

"Perfect," George said. "Those four will freak out pretty fast."

"Yeah," Wally agreed.

"So what are we? George asked. "Wolves or coyotes or owls?"

"I make great owl hoots," Yan said, and he proceeded to demonstrate in a muted voice. It sounded pretty eerie.

"I can yip pretty well," Wally said, and he gave a few experimental yips.

"Count me in as the howler," George added, and he gave one long, lonely wolf howl.

"So what do you want to do?" George asked Ricky.

"I don't know," Ricky said. He really didn't have his heart in this.

Wally thought for a minute, and then said, "I got it. When we make noises, the girls are sure to rush to the window and look out. You go stand on the window side of the cabin where they can see you and be a ghost."

"A ghost?" Ricky said. "How do I do that?"

"Remember that old sheet you found in the bottom dresser drawer? Use it to cover yourself up. With a flashlight beneath, shining out, it'll look pretty good. Let's try it out."

Wally took the old sheet out of the drawer and draped it over Ricky, covering his head and most of his face. Ricky clutched it in place with one hand, while holding a flashlight in the other hand and letting it shine out from underneath.

"Not half bad," Yan said, admiring their handiwork. "Ghostly sounds, please." Yan tapped Ricky on the head as he spoke, and Ricky began to wail.

"Excellent," Wally agreed. "And if they start to come out of the cabin, we run for it. But don't come straight back here. We don't want them to know we came from Cabin Six. Scatter in the dark and sneak back here as fast as you can."

The four boys left quietly and made their way through the trees to Cabin Twelve. Ricky hadn't turned on his flashlight yet, but he crept close to the girls' cabin on the window side and took up a position there. The air was suddenly rent with hoots, yips, and howls. Lights immediately came on not only in Cabin Twelve but in Cabin Eleven, too. As Wally predicted, faces appeared at the Butterfly cabin window. Ricky flipped on his flashlight and began to shriek and moan and weave back and forth.

One face disappeared from the window and then jerkily returned. Ricky felt pretty sure it was Annabelle hopping on one foot. Ricky heard the sound of the window being pushed open. It was time to retreat. Before he got more than a step away, he felt the shock of cold water running down his head and back. Annabelle had thrown a glass of water at him with deadly aim.

Ricky turned off the flashlight and made for the woods. His brother owl, coyote, and wolf were racing through the darkness, too. Each went in a roundabout way, but all made it back about the same time to Cabin Six and stood just inside the door, breathing hard.

"Don't turn on the light," George whispered. "None of the boys' cabins have their lights on."

"Ditch that sheet, Ricky," Wally said, "in case someone comes around."

"Glad to," Ricky said, jerking it off. "It's all wet. One of those girls – I think it was Annabelle – threw a glass of water at me." The others laughed at that news. Ricky dried off his hair and then rolled up the sheet and stuck it back in the bottom drawer.

Hearing voices, the four went outside in the darkness in front of their cabin. Several boys were there from the Rattlers and Grizzlies cabins.

As they milled about, one of the Rattlers asked, "What's going on?"

"I don't know," Yan said innocently. "Probably just the girls imagining something."

They heard some adult voices in the distance up by the girls' cabins that sounded like Mr. Bennett and Mrs. Hannigan. Before long, things grew quiet again, and cabin lights went out one by one.

In Owl Cabin, the boys sat on their bunks laughing softly and feeling proud of themselves.

Soon they settled into their bunks. Ricky heard the steady rhythm of his friends' breathing as one by one they fell asleep. He tossed for quite a while from side to side. He kept thinking, another whole day had passed, and half the night, and still no Bones. Would his dog be missing for good? In the quiet darkness of the cabin, a tear trickled down Ricky's cheek.

CHAPTER 22

Everyone laughed and talked next morning at breakfast in the main lodge about the goings on of the night before. Ricky nibbled at his food and sat twisting his paper napkin at first, expecting any minute to be found out for their tricks on the Butterflies. It turned out, though, that the wild animals and the ghost that surrounded Cabin Twelve were only a part of the after-dark activities. Someone had thrown rolls of toilet paper over another one of the girls' cabins, and it took quite a while this morning to clean it up.

Although there was a lot of talk as to who might have done what, and why, that was all it was—talk.

Yan, Wally, George, and Ricky innocently joined in making guesses, but they never let on about their own part in last night's adventures. It soon became delightfully clear that there was no way they'd be found guilty of their ghostly escapade. The only evidence against them was a still-damp sheet hidden away in a bottom drawer. No one had any reason to look there.

Ricky's last activity was to work with microscopes and pond water. This had all been set up in a basement room. The students looked at a variety of water samples. In one, Ricky saw some protozoa covered in hundreds of hairs moving through the water. In another he saw one with a whip-like tail.

He observed but had little to say to anyone. When it was finally over, grimly silent and lead-footed, Ricky took part in the final group hike.

All Ricky wanted was to be finished here at Camp Betasso and get back to town to hunt for his dog. At last all their stuff was packed up and stowed in the back of the bus, and they began the drive home. Ricky sat by the window again, and when they reached the edge of Broomfield, he kept scanning for a stray dog.

The bus drove down the main street of town, where everything looked familiar to Ricky. He glanced up one of the side streets and caught a glimpse of the playground of his old school. He felt a little pang of loss, but not a big one. Now that he'd made some friends and had met the teachers at Mesa, he was starting to feel okay about it.

Two blocks farther on, he recognized the sign for the street where he had lived. He looked down it, wondering if the people who'd moved into his old house were still keeping an eye out for Bones. It was probably silly to think his dog would come walking all the way back to Broomfield. But even as he thought that, Ricky had the sensation that Bones was not far away.

The bus turned onto Lincoln Avenue, leading to the turnpike that would take them back to Boulder. Ricky had about given up hope, but he couldn't stop himself from continuing to look out the window. He watched a small poodle on a leash being walked by an old lady, and he saw a big Labrador, sniffing at a garbage pail.

Mile after mile went by. Finally they pulled into the parking lot of Mesa School. The cars of parents who'd come to pick up their children jammed the parking lot. As their bus drove in, Ricky saw a knot of people standing at the drop off point. George's mother waved, and Ricky's mother was standing next to her. Then he picked out Mike's car.

Mr. Bennett's bus had arrived just ahead of theirs, and Annabelle had already limped over to her dad's car. Ricky saw Mike get out to help as Annabelle opened the car door and he heard her shriek. What was happening? Ricky joined his mother and they hurried to the car. Ricky saw Annabelle in the back seat hugging Darwin.

"Look!" Annabelle cried, holding up her precious bundle for Ricky to admire. "Darwin's well enough to be home again."

As Mike stowed their camping gear in the trunk, Ricky's mother explained. "We picked up Darwin this morning,"

In spite of the hole in his own heart, Ricky felt happiness for Annabelle. Darwin was safe and home again. Only Bones was missing.

Mike carefully maneuvered the car out of the busy lot. "Darwin's a little sedated and sleepy now, but the vet said he's doing great."

"He's perfect," Annabelle said.

"He needs a little more healing before he's completely well," Mike went on, "so we have to keep an eye on him and not let him wander far."

Ricky thought the vet really didn't need to worry. Annabelle looked as if she'd never let go of her cat again, and a drowsy Darwin seemed perfectly content to sit in her lap.

As she prepared and served lunch, Ricky's mom talked to him about Bones. "With the piece in the paper and a picture on Facebook, I'm hoping someone will soon have news of Bones. Other than wait, I'm not sure what we can do."

"There is one thing," Ricky said. "I want to search the area near our old house in Broomfield. As we drove by in the bus this morning, I really did think Bones was nearby. Could we go there, Mom? Please?"

Maria looked at Ricky. "Yes," she said. "After lunch I'll drive us out there. It's worth a try."

As soon as lunch was over, Ricky and his mother prepared to leave.

"I'll come, too," Mike said.

"Darwin needs to rest, and Annabelle should be with him," Ricky's mom said. "So you should be here with them."

"You don't know the Broomfield trails like I do," Ricky added. "I just want to check out the paths near our old house. You should stay here with Annabelle and Darwin."

Ricky managed to tell his mother a little about the weekend as they drove to Broomfield.

"Mark did call and tell me how sorry he was not to be able to come up and give the magic show, but he's promised to schedule a performance at the school for free next month," his mother said.

Once in Broomfield, Ricky and his mother stopped at the old house. The new owners invited them in. Seeing others' furniture in their old familiar home seemed strange to Ricky. They didn't stay long, but left and started walking a few of the familiar paths. No sign of Bones.

"Where else should we look?" Ricky's mom asked.

"About the only place we haven't tried is the Rough and Ready Ditch Trail," Ricky said. It starts down at the Baptist Church and goes all the way up to the school playground. Bones and I have hiked it a lot."

They saw nothing unusual as they walked up the trail. Then Ricky noticed a spot where the grass as the side of the creek was packed down. It looked as if an animal might have slept there. Ricky went over for a closer look. In the damp ground, he saw dog footprints. Ricky's heart began to beat faster. Of course he couldn't tell for sure, but these prints were definitely the right size. Could it be?

Ricky reported what he had seen to his mother, and then he ran up the path.

Ricky ran fast, breathing hard. It might seem silly, but somehow, he sensed that Bones was not far away. The thought made his run even faster. Up ahead, near the bridge that crossed the creek, Ricky saw something. A dog!

"Bones!" Ricky yelled. "Bones!"

The dog stopped and turned his head. Then like a flash he raced back to Ricky. Ricky dropped to his knees and hugged his dog tight. Bones' tail wagged super fast, beating a tattoo on the path. Bones licked away the salty tears of joy that were running down Ricky's face.

Ricky picked up his dog, who had grown so thin, Ricky could feel his ribs. Then, ignoring an unpleasant smell, he clutched his precious dog close, and he hurried back down the path. He could see his mother jogging toward them.

Ricky, his mother, and Bones sat together in a heap at the side of the path and laughed and cried together.

Finally, they all went back down the path to where the car was parked and got inside. Ricky and Bones sat in the back seat. Ricky's Mom called Mike to share the good news and then they headed home.

As soon as the car drove in the garage, Mike came out to meet them. There was another round of hugs.

"I wonder what adventures that dog's had. He went a long way. How did he ever get all the way back there?" Mike asked.

"I wish he could tell us," Ricky's mother said.

Annabelle, still holding Darwin, came over and patted Bones. "Welcome home," she said. "And here's Darwin who's home, too. He wants to thank you for saving him." Annabelle took Darwin's paw and patted Bones on the head with it.

Bones' tail thumped loudly.

"He needs a good dinner and a bath," Ricky's mother said.

Ricky let go of Bones long enough to fill a bowl with food and another with water. He stood close by watching Bones wolf the food down. Bones' fur was caked with dried mud.

Then Ricky opened the door and let Bones into the yard. "You're a mess," he said, "and you need a good bath. I'll change my clothes and be out in a minute."

Ricky stepped back into the house.

Annabelle said, "I'm so glad Bones isn't missing anymore."

"Me, too," Ricky said, and then stared in amazement as Bones suddenly appeared at his feet, wagging his tail. "How did you..." Ricky stopped and looked at the spot where the old cat door had been. It had been replaced with a new door, plenty big enough for Bones.

Ricky looked at Mike. "Thanks," he said.

Ricky sat down on the floor right in front of the pet door and burrowed his face into Bones' still muddy fur. Then he looked up and grinned at his mom, Mike, Annabelle and Darwin and hugged his dog again as he said, "We fit now, don't we, Bones."

About the Author

Phyllis J. Perry grew up in northern California and was graduated from the University of California, Berkeley. She and her husband and two daughters moved to Colorado where Phyllis received her doctorate degree from the University of Colorado, and worked as a teacher, curriculum specialist, elementary school principal and Director of Talented & Gifted Education for the Boulder Valley Schools. Phyllis now writes full time for children and adults. She lives in Boulder, not far from Rocky Mountain National Park which has been the subject for a number of her nonfiction books.

ACKNOWLEDGMENTS

The author expresses deep appreciation to the following who offered expertise, support and encouragement throughout the writing of this book:

David Perry

Penny Noyce

Barnas Monteith

Yu-Yi Ling

and to Ravenwood's Brass Bugle,
the beagle who provided the inspiration.

Tumblehome Learning's NSTA-CBC OSTB Award (Outstanding Science Trade Books K-12) Winning Titles

Juvenile Fiction

Mosquitoes Don't Bite Me (2017)
978-1-943431-30-4
978-1-943431-37-3

The Walking Fish (2015)
978-0-9907829-3-3
978-0-9907829-4-0

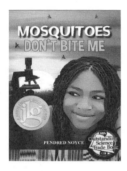

Something Stinks! (2013)
978-0-9850008-9-9

Young Adult Non-Fiction

Magnificent Minds (2015)
978-0-9897924-7-9
978-1-943431-25-0

*Remarkable Minds (*2015)
978-0-9907829-0-2
978-1-943431-13-7

Other Tumblehome Learning Titles

Non-Fiction Reads

Inventors, Makers, Barrier Breakers (2018) 978-1-943431-42-7

I Wondered About That Too (2018) 978-1-943431-38-0

I Always Wondered About That - 101 Questions And Answers About Science & Other Stuff (2017) 978-1-943431-29-8

Dinosaur Eggs & Blue Ribbons (2015) 978-0-9897924-5-5

Fiction

Jake And The Quake (2018) 978-1-943431-39-7, 978-1-943431-40-3

Seven Stories About The Moon (science poetry, 2018) 978-1-943431-33-5

Missing Bones (2018) 978-1-943431-34-2

TimeTilter (2018) 978-1-943431-31-1

Gasparilla's Gold (2016) 978-1-943431-19-9, 978-1-943431-20-5

Bees On The Roof (2018) 978-1-943431-24-3

Bees On The Roof (2016) 978-1-943431-21-2, 978-1-943431-22-9

Talk To Me (2016) 978-1-943431-23-6

Picture Books

Waiting for Joey - Studying Penguins in Antarctica (2018) 978-1-943431-41-0

How the Dormacks Evolved Longer Backs (2018) 978-1-943431-27-4

Geology Is A Piece Of Cake (2017) 978-1-943431-28-1

How the Piloses Evolved Skinny Noses (2017) 978-1-943431-26-7

Stem Cells Are Everywhere (2016) 978-0-9897924-9-3

Seeking the Snow Leopard (2016) 978-1-943431-16-8

Painting In The Dark - Esref Armagan, Blind Artist (2016) 978-1-943431-15-1, 978-1-943431-14-4

Elizabeth's Constellation Quilt (2015) 978-0-9907829-1-9

GALACTIC ACADEMY OF SCIENCE, "G.A.S.", SERIES

CLINTON AND MAE'S MISSIONS:

The Desperate Case of the Diamond Chip
978-0-9850008-0-6
The Vicious Case of the Viral Vaccine
978-0-9850008-7-5
The Baffling Case of the Battered Brain
978-0-9897924-1-7
The Perilous Case of the Zombie Potion
978-0-9897924-3-1
The Contaminated Case of the Cooking Contest
978-0-9907829-2-6
The Secret Case of the Space Station Stowaways
978-1-943431-18-2

ANITA AND BENSON'S MISSIONS:

The Furious Case of the Fraudulent Fossil
978-0-9850008-5-1
The Harrowing Case of the Hackensack Hacker
978-0-9850008-8-2
The Confounding Case of the Climate Crisis
978-0-9897924-4-8

ELLA AND SHOMARI'S MISSION:

The Cryptic Case of the Coded Fair
978-0-9897924-2-4